THE CORRIDOR

THE CORRIDOR

A New Danger Has Arrived in the Everglades

Tom McGrath

Cover Photo of Big Cypress Swamp by Tom McGrath
Author Photo by Laura McGrath

For Marlo

*May the corridors in your life lead you
to more wonderful experiences than you can even imagine.*

PROLOGUE

Jake Ballard and Al Jordan had been paddling for what seemed like forever. The sun beat down relentlessly, the heat was overwhelming, and the surrounding water felt just a few degrees south of steam. They had left Chokoloskee Island in the cooler dawn and headed south, zigzagging among all the small keys, past the Lopez River outfall to Lumber Island in the 10,000 Islands of the western Everglades. Like most of the islands here, Lumber is covered in a dense stand of mangroves. But unlike many, it has a sand and shell beach facing west that could handle camping gear. Gulf breezes were possible. They might make things more comfortable and keep down the mosquitos and no-see-ums. Maybe not. Setting up camp before darkness was a priority, though. There was little ambient light out here and there would be no moon this night. Lots of kayakers came out this way, particularly to neighboring Rabbit Key, in the cooler months. But this was early summer, and the heat and humidity had started in with a vengeance.

Jake, a professor at Florida Gulf Coast University and a volunteer on this project, was working with Al who was part of a Florida Fish and Wildlife group surveying the fringes of the Everglades for habitat diversity. He was looking for invasive plants that might destroy what was left of natural wilderness here. Jake was here for a couple of weeks just before launching into his summer season of field research with his students. Al was a botanist. Ridding this place from destructive invasives that were ripping old Florida to pieces was his passion. Both he and

Al had worked with teams of other scientists and citizen volunteers surveying many of the fragmented remnants of Florida's wild places for their department, the Nature Conservancy, Audubon, and other organizations. In these national park islands they could see some of the places where destruction wasn't as bad as it was in areas more accessible to the gold coast megacity.

They had purposely chosen to stay away from the elevated thatched platforms called chickees set up by the National Park Service for camping in the Glades. Every winter season, people who kayaked twice a year at most launched themselves into this wild area and got lost, burned to a crisp, dehydrated, or bitten to the point of becoming a single large insect bite. They also left behind a trail of trash that they should have carried out with them when they left the backcountry. These two wanted no part of that. So beach camping was their best option. Jake and Al found a nice stretch of sand for a camp bordered by mangroves on the Gulf side of Lumber. Luckily, tonight the breeze was good and steady out of the west. The bonus was that this beach was out of cell phone coverage so a quiet night with no intrusions was ahead.

After setting up the camp and wolfing down what passed for dinner, they sat in their camp chairs and reviewed what they had seen that day. By 9:00 pm they decided to call it a night and get an early and cooler start in the morning. Al took his flashlight and headed down the beach that ended at the mangroves saying, "Got to see a man. Be back in a bit." Jake decided to finish a few notes he had started earlier using his headlamp for light. Moments later he heard a crash down where Al had headed. It sounded loud for a man just wandering in the bush. Maybe he had fallen. "Al?" he called. No answer. "Al, you OK?" he tried again. Still no answer.

Jake picked up his flashlight for extra light and headed down the beach where he had seen Al's light disappear. "Al, you back there?" he called when he got to the mangroves. No sound and no sign. Jake scanned the undergrowth with his light. Then he turned the light to the beach and the water. Just at the edge of some black mangrove pneumatophores he saw the flashlight. It was off and in the water. Still there was no sign of Al. The more he called, the less he seemed to hear as the insects and small night creatures quieted down with his noise.

Jake moved around as best he could, swinging the flashlight in an arc. It didn't penetrate the vegetation very deeply but it was clear from what he could make out that Al was nowhere near where he was standing. He felt his heartrate climb as the realization took hold that Al was no longer anywhere close by. He retrieved the discarded light and headed back to the camp. No sign, no sound. Jake couldn't sleep but he couldn't do much to search for Al either. Not until daylight. He hoped that somehow Al would find his way back to camp. In the meantime Jake just kept calling out every now and then, hoping to get an answer. None came.

When dawn finally brought light to the camp, Jake headed back down the beach and into the mangroves. Not a single sign that Al had been there. Back on the beach he found what he suspected were Al's footprints in the sand. He tried to follow them into the mangroves. He lost them quickly. Jake was no tracker.

After an hour of futility Jake took a GPS reading for the camp, left his gear, and headed out in his kayak to the nearest place he thought he could get a phone signal to call in help. People just don't disappear like that. Not here. They were away from big animal predators. There wasn't quicksand or sink holes here to swallow people up. This kind of thing just didn't happen out here. But it had.

1

Shelly Lawson was the best re-constructor in the museum. She could use a bone fragment from almost any vertebrate alive or fossilized and build a three-dimensional model of what that body part had looked like in nature. She knew the ins and outs of ligament attachment, joint structures and muscle mass all over the body for almost everything with a backbone that had ever been alive. What she stared at now, however, was a crude cast and a few pictures of what was claimed to be a very partial paw print from a fairly large animal. Not the kind of material she was used to working with. Whoever had decided that what she had in front of her was evidence of any kind, had to have a really vivid imagination.

She had been asked to see if she could re-create a more complete print from these few pieces of information so that the animal that made it could be identified. The cast and pictures had been made in some way out place called the Ten Thousand Islands in Florida. Shelly had a vague recollection of having heard of them once but really had little idea of where they were or even what part of Florida they were in. Apparently some guy had gone missing there. The only thing the search and rescue crew had found that might be a clue was this "partial print" in the sandy marl near where he had disappeared. This after a three day search of the whole densely covered island where he and his friend had camped. The crew had searched three neighboring islands too. They had even used infrared sensors and photo-drones in the search.

Since there was no evidence that people other than the two scientists had been in the area for days if not weeks, initial speculation among the various search teams was that some big animal had somehow taken the guy without a trace. But the habitat was wrong for those.

The disappearance had been on an island in salt or at least brackish water. Alligators don't like saltwater. And even though they often grow big enough to attack and kill people, most of the time it was small dogs and children they went after unless some hapless golfer came too close to one in order to prevent having to take an extra stroke for a lost ball. Panthers don't like salt water either and are almost exclusively dry land animals. Panthers, or really the cougars that lived in parts of Florida, were smallish and rarely seen. Reports of attacks on humans in Florida were non-existent. Sure, cougars out west sometimes would attack and even kill a human. But there are only about 150 of these cats left in the wilds of the Everglades and Big Cypress and they try very hard to stay away from people.

If a big animal were to be suspected, that left the possibility of the American Crocodile. They like salt water, are found in the area the search teams were working in, and got really big. In fact, a 700 pound one was captured off the coast near Tarpon Springs north of Tampa/St. Petersburg just a year or so earlier. The problem is they don't eat large prey and have never been reported to attack a human in Florida. Besides, what she could make of the print in front of her didn't look likely to be a print made by a claw.

The cast Shelly was working on had been made under water, shallow sea water based on the report that came with it. The pictures were mostly photographs which were cloudy, having been taken through several inches of murky water. The few drawings were carefully made and the measurements taken were clear but there really wasn't a great deal to go on. No part of the print was whole, and it wasn't even clear that all of what was visible was part of a single print to begin with.

She had shown the images and descriptions to a few others in the museum who knew animal prints. No one was able to help and the few who made suggestions were just taking wild guesses. The guy who had suggested a giant sloth or a cave bear should have gotten a laugh but for some reason no one in the lab found his suggestions funny.

Shelly started by outlining the parts of the cast she could determine might be valid pieces of the print. She then used a computer graphics program that automatically continued the outlines in several likely directions. She thought if she could get a small part of the print re-created she might be able to make some better guesses as to how to fill it out. Then she could try to match what she created with known paw prints or tracks of living animals.

Several bits of what might have been part of the print seemed way too far apart for a track from any animal in the Everglades that she could think of. That might mean that what she was looking at was more than one print or not part of a print at all.

She set up the algorithm for repeated trials on the few parts she decided to work on and let the computer do its work. It was time to head home anyway. It was a long subway ride to Brooklyn but luckily she had worked late enough to avoid the worst of rush hour. But dinner would have to be takeout, one more time.

2

Jake Ballard was frustrated. Al Jordan had been a long-time friend and colleague. Jake had worked with Al on a bunch of field studies and knew he was a dedicated and careful field scientist. He would know about all the possible problems that he could encounter on an island in the Gulf and how to avoid them. His disappearance right in front of him without any clues as to why seemed impossible to imagine. The fact that not a single bit of solid evidence was found for any scenario was maddening.

Jake had met Al when he first came to Florida a decade and a half ago. They formed an instant bond over science and a few beers. Jake had just filed for divorce from his wife, who still lived up in Madison, Wisconsin. Al had never been married but he seemed to know just what to say and do for Jake when things got tough.

He and Al had first worked together as part of a team that surveyed and then traveled through what had been called the Florida Wildlife Corridor. This had been a long hoped for salvation for wild Florida. It meant connecting wild lands from the Keys to the Georgia border. Wildlife corridors had been developed in the United States and Canada, Europe, South America, and from India to Bhutan and had been found to really revitalize areas where habitat fragmentation through urbanization and human development had all but destroyed wild lands. This one was hard to develop, though, since it had to go under major roads like Alligator Alley and over canals and rivers to allow populations of animals and plants to interbreed. That was the only way to slow down the disaster of species loss that seemed destined for Florida and keep enough genetic diversity in the system so it didn't self-destruct anyway.

Al had been delighted to find so many different species of his beloved native plants in abundance during that work. He had been rabid about ridding the state of invasives like Melaleuca, Brazilian Pepper, and Australian pine. He knew it was a losing battle, just as the battles against water lettuce and hydrilla had been, but he never quit hoping it would get better. From his point of view this corridor business had the best potential for progress by preventing the reproductive isolation of native plants thus hastening their decline.

Jake had taken a sabbatical from Florida Gulf Coast University to work with Al for that year. They had published some papers together, but more importantly, they had become close friends. He wanted some answers, and soon.

Jake had stayed on to work with the search and rescue team as long as he could before heading out to his field research site. After a week, the search and rescue team had recovered only one possible clue, what they thought might be a partial paw print from Lumber Island. From Jake's perspective it seemed way too long without an answer from Jake's perspective. None of the search team had any experience in how to go about reconstruction themselves. They sent what they collected up to Gainesville expecting someone at the museum there to be able to identify the print. It hadn't taken more than two days before word came back that the museum people were forwarding the collected material up the Museum of Natural History in New York City to someone who was said to be fantastic, maybe the best, at piecing this kind of partial evidence together. So much for that.

Jake had had enough of waiting around. He decided to call this expert in New York and see what she was finding. He had gotten Shelly's name from a friend in Gainesville, and it wasn't hard to track down her number. He wasn't going to mess with email or text messages. Those communications were just too easy to ignore. Just ask anybody who tried communicating that way with contractors in Florida, for instance. You never got an answer.

"Hi Ms. Lawson. My name is Jake Ballard at Florida Gulf Coast University. I'm a friend of the guy who went missing in the Ten Thousand Islands. I was with him when he disappeared, and I'm really anxious to find out what you have on that partial they sent you. We need some answers down here."

"Well Dr. Ballard, I can't say I have anything really," Shelly replied hesitantly. How much information she should give out over the phone to someone she didn't know was a worrisome question. She had gotten the material and the request from the museum people at the University of Florida, not Gulf Coast whatever. Maybe this was a ruse from some reporter trying to get a scoop. Time to be cautious here.

"Do you mean you've come up empty or you're just not done with the analysis yet?" Jake asked.

"Well, I'm pretty far along, but I can't say there is anything I can really share at the moment. Give me your contact information and I'll get back to you when I wrap this up better," Shelly replied.

If he gave her enough information she could track him down and find out if he was legitimate enough to share what she found with him.

"Can you tell me where you are in the process at least and how long it might be before we hear about what you find?" Jake asked.

"I wish I knew how far along I was in the process, Dr. Ballard, but since I don't know what I'm really looking for, I can't really say how close I've come to finding the answer. Just give me your contact information and I'll get back to you when I get something I can share." Shelly was starting to get annoyed. Why would this guy just call out of the blue when she'd never heard of him before anyway?

Jake could hear her frustration and he realized that he was going to get nowhere with this conversation. He got Shelly's email address and hung up. He quickly sent her his contact information and some information about himself and some references to papers he and Al had written together so she would know he was not just a curious sideliner. If she looked at a few of the papers she would know just how good a scientist Al was. Maybe that would kick her into higher gear on this. It just might be possible that he was even more frustrated now than before he talked to this Lawson person.

3

Shelly put down the phone a little too hard and looked down at the stack of what seemed to be junk drawings that her computer had generated overnight. She thought maybe if she hung them on the wall and got some distance from them something might jump out for her that hadn't when she was looking at them at arms' length. Once she had the images taped up, she stepped back. Nothing new popped off the pages.

As she started to take it all down Randy, the intern from down the hall, stuck his head in her lab and asked if he could borrow one of her reconstruction tools. He got a surprised look on his face as he scanned the array of images on the wall.

"What kind of cat made those prints?" he asked.

"Wait," said Shelly. "Where do you see anything that looks like cat prints?"

"Right here and some of this here, too." Randy replied pointing to two renditions not far from each other on the wall. "If these are life size, it looks like a big mother, too."

While Shelly felt a little taken aback that she hadn't seen the possible prints herself, she was glad to have had them pointed out. Now she could see why Randy had reacted the way he had. They weren't complete or a hundred percent clear, but there was enough there to believe that what she was looking at were paw prints from a really big cat.

"You're right!" Shelly exclaimed. "If these renditions are the real thing, we are probably looking at something that isn't supposed to be where these were found. Do you remember hearing about the guy who disappeared in some islands off the coast of Florida a while ago without a trace?"

"Yeah, I remember hearing something about that."

"Well these drawings were computer-generated possible reconstructions of whole prints starting with some very sketchy partials that were sent up here from that site where he disappeared."

"The only cat of any size I know about in Florida is the panther and it isn't all that big," said Randy. "What are you gonna do with these renditions?"

"I think you and I are going to take them down the hall to mammology and get some opinions from the people there," Shelly said, grabbing the most obvious drawings off the wall and ushering Randy out the door.

"Hey, Phil. Gotta a minute to look at a couple of drawings?" Shelly asked as they walked into the mammology department lab and found the department head poring over some very small bones on a black velvet cloth.

"Sure, for you, Shelly." Phil replied.

As Phil took the drawings and started to look closely at them Shelly filled in the story of how they were made and how Randy had been the first to see that they might represent prints from some known animal. She also made sure to tell Phil that the prints were sized based on the measurements taken in the field. She didn't mention anything about Randy's speculation that they belonged to a big cat, hoping not to bias any call he made about them.

"They look like cat prints of some kind, but they are way too big to be anything I know of from the Americas." Phil said after a couple of minutes of consideration. "Give me about a half hour to track down some possibilities and I'll get back to you."

Shelly and Randy went back to her lab, both too interested in what Phil might turn up to get back to work on anything else. They went back through the remaining drawings hoping to find even more that they hadn't noticed before. Nothing showed itself.

"You guys aren't going to believe this, and I don't either by the way, but the closest I can get to anything from those drawings is a tiger. Based on the size here I'd say it would be about 500 pounds, too. Probably not a very good mouser," Phil said as he strode into the reconstruction lab.

"Well I don't believe that!" said Shelly.

"How much do you trust the computer that generated this stuff?" asked Phil.

"I thought I trusted it a lot but with this I'm not at all sure," Shelly replied.

"What happens next?" asked Randy.

"We'll file a report and move on to something else since this clearly isn't likely to be real. They'll have to blame that disappearance on flying saucer abduction I guess," said Shelly. "Thanks for trying, Phil."

"All righty then," said Randy walking out of the lab with Phil and feeling let down by findings.

Shelly spent the next day and a half trying to find just the right way to write up these outcomes. She sure as hell didn't want to sound very positive about the prints being made by a tiger. She also didn't want to completely bury that idea either. She did trust her computer program to have given her the most likely rendition of a complete print and she really trusted Randy's eye. She had seen his work from the beginning of his internship and it was stellar. She would certainly give him a lot of credit for their taking the reconstructions to Phil. This was the hardest report she ever had to write in spite of it being very short.

4

Jake threw the report from Shelly Lawson down on the steamer trunk that served as his coffee table. How could she have come up with such trash from what the team had sent her? This had to be bogus. What kind of foolish algorithm did she use in that computer anyway?

If this was the best they could do with the only pieces of evidence they had, he was going to have to come to grips with the idea that no answer was out there about Al. He just wasn't ready to do that. He had brought the report home with him because he wanted one more careful look at it before he resigned himself to the inevitable. It was going to take at least two beers, though, before he could get back into that report.

Jake took a quick shower and plunked himself down in the rocker that he used to calm himself at the end of rough days. The first beer went down very fast. Before he cracked the second one he had calmed down enough to know that he hadn't paid close enough attention to the details in his first read through. He picked up the report and dove in one more time.

An hour later he was still no less frustrated by the findings. With the report suggesting something so patently ridiculous, he knew the case would be put aside by everyone involved now. There was nothing more to do. The second beer sat warm and unopened beside him. He put the report aside and went to find that bottle of scotch he thought he needed now. It would keep him company through the evening and he could toast his missing friend.

5

Field work in the middle of a Florida summer is not the most comfortable. Heat and humidity are unrelenting, and rains almost every day bring out hoards of insects. Jake had only the summers to get his field work done. He had too big a teaching and advising load to consider doing any of that during the school year. So he had devised his research so that data collection happened in the summer. He used student helpers in the field whenever he could find the right ones. During the rest of the year he put his best and brightest in the lab back home working on the data they collected.

This late June weather was not the worst of it, but it was certainly bad enough out here. He and two 19 year olds were waist deep in a slough surrounded by sawgrass; they were all sweating like there were a faucets in their pores. Why would the damn cell phone in his safari shirt be ringing now? Everyone knew he was out here. He only carried the thing in case of emergency, not so the rest of the world could stay in touch.

"Hey Jake. This is Steve Hamilton from Everglades National Park. We worked a bit together on that search for the guy who disappeared on Lumber Key last month."

Had it really been almost a month since that search for Al? The loss was still palpable to Jake.

"Yeah Steve. I remember you. What's up?" Jake asked.

"We got a rather strange report from up near the Tamiami not far from the reservation." Steve said referring to the Miccosukee Village area. "Actually it was near the Shark Valley Visitor's center."

"Why are you calling me about this one, Steve?" Jake asked, curious as to why anyone would call him about a report to the National Park Service.

"The guy who we interviewed swears he saw a really big orange and black striped cat-like thing near the observation tower there. I remembered you were the one most interested in what the museum people reported back from the little bit of evidence we collected from Lumber Key, and this sighting took me back to that report. I thought you might be interested in helping us look into this guy's claim," said Steve.

Yeah right, thought Jake. Just what I need to do is give up time from the field and chase down some delusional guy's swamp dream. Hell, Shark Valley was like 50 or more miles away from Lumber Key as the crow flies. He just wasn't sure he was up to a wild goose chase on this one. Delusional guy sees big cat in swamp. Still….

"Lemme get back to you, Steve," Jake replied. "I'll see if I can arrange to get away."

Not answering outright would give him time to think about whether he wanted any part of their nonsense and time to arrange for work to continue without him if he decided he did want to join the search.

During the rest of the day he talked to his students about the work they were all doing and got very comfortable with their abilities to carry on without him as long as he stayed in touch. The more he thought about that museum report, the more he found that he was talking himself into joining the National Park and Fish and Wildlife team.

He punched the recall button. Steve picked up on the fourth ring. "I can do it, Steve. When do you want me and where should I go?" Jake asked.

"See you tomorrow about 10:00 at the Shark Valley Center. We'll start looking from there for the animal, if he did see one. Glad you're going to be with us," Steve said as he hung up.

For the rest of the afternoon Jake worked with the students, laying out the work they would be doing on their own for the next few days. He was sure this folly wasn't going to take more than a couple of days, and he expected to be back on his field site right after the weekend. He was already packed for the field, so not much to do there. Just get on the road early enough to be at Shark Valley by10:00.

6

Everglades National Park's Shark Valley Visitor Center is off the Tamiami Trail, Rt. 41, just east of the Miccosukee Village. It could be a busy place in the cooler months since the Miccosukee offer airboat tours of the Glades from near the Center, where they have their own visitor center and restaurant. The National Park Center rented bikes and ran tram tours on the 15 miles of road that go into the Glades from there. Easy biking on flat roads make it great for families.

Now it was late June and almost empty. Who wants to bike in a swamp when the heat index is over 100 with all that humidity? At least one guy did. He was a German tourist who came there specifically because of the heat and humidity. He loved it. He had fulfilled his dream of being alone in the Everglades when he biked the Shark Valley Loop Road. He had gone out about noon and the 2:00 pm tram tour had been cancelled because no one showed up for it due to the heat. He hadn't imagined when he asked at the Center what he might have seen out there in the Glades that he would be put in a room and literally interrogated. He was supposed to be on his way to the naturist beaches of the Gold Coast for a week of sandy, mostly naked fun in the sun. The question he asked after his bike ride was really putting a dent in his time. Everyone wanted to talk to him, it seemed.

He had described to the park and Fish and Wildlife people what he had seen. It wasn't much. He just wanted someone to tell him what it might have been. He had gotten off his bike at the observation tower at the southern end of the loop and scanned the Glades that spread out in what seemed like an endless panorama from there. Not more than a few birds were moving anywhere, and it was mostly silent except for some wind in the trees and sawgrass.

For just the briefest time, maybe only a second, he caught something out of the corner of his left eye that moved like his pet cat. Whatever it was seemed really big, though. The only thing he made out was some color. It had looked orangish to him, much like his orange tabby back home with maybe some black on it or a dark shadow here and there. But it had come into his field of vision and left so fast he couldn't be sure.

Now he was back for a second day with a new group of "interrogators." The "Doberman" among them was some guy named Jack or Jock or Jake or something. He really didn't care. He just wanted that guy out of his face. He had told them everything, and it took all he had in him not to make things up just to get them off his case so he could be on his way.

Once they had their fill of his story they took his contact information and let him leave. They had put him up in a fairly nice place in Ft. Lauderdale and given him enough money for a good meal and a few beers. It didn't seem enough.

After the German was out of the Center, Jake and the people from the park and Fish and Wildlife sat down at a table and worked through a plan to search the area of the reported sighting. They knew that whatever had been there would be long gone, but maybe, just maybe, it had left some more conclusive evidence behind.

Jake understood why they had called him when he heard the German's story. It sounded like the guy may have seen a tiger, and Jake had been more than dismissive of the report from that Lawson woman in New York. Here might be a chance to confirm her hypotheses or mount some compelling evidence against it.

The team of six headed down to the Loop Road to the tower. They had decided to walk into the Glades from the road near the tower in widening concentric arcs about an arm's length apart until they had covered about 1000 yard radius semicircle.

There was no chance for prints here since where they were walking was a wet prairie of sawgrass. The whole area was underwater since the wet season had begun and afternoon rains and storms were occurring almost daily. What they hoped to find was maybe some fur or leftover food. Anything that could give them more concrete information than the sighting report.

"Man, this sawgrass is nasty," said Jake, not far into the first search loop.

"Yeah, but that works in our favor if the saw teeth on the grass pulls off some fur or scratches whatever was out here," Sam from F&W pointed out. Luckily they were all in long sleeves and heavy pants for just that reason.

About a half hour into the search Ellen, a park ranger from the Shark Valley center, who was walking on the outside edge of the team deepest into the Glades shouted, "Hold up! I've got something here."

She took a glycine envelope out of her shirt pocket and got out her Swiss Army knife. It had tweezers. She was also carrying a small bottle of alcohol which she used to sterilize the tweezers. They each had been carrying the same equipment just in case this kind of thing turned up. Jake and the others stood as still as they could and watched Ellen carefully pull some thready material from the edge of a sawgrass blade just to her left. She placed it in the envelope, closed the flap and folded it over, marked it #1 with a Sharpie she was carrying and tucked it back in her shirt. One of the other searchers took a GPS reading and saved it.

"Well that's something. Hope we find more." Jake said.

Two hours later they were finished. No more was found.

7

Why the hell did they send this sample of hair up here? Shelly asked herself. There were perfectly capable people at the University of Florida and the museum there. Besides, why had her supervisor put her on this sample rather than one of the mammal people at the museum?

But she knew why. She just didn't like it that she was on the line again with this one. First of all she had been the one to write the report claiming the print she had analyzed from Lumber Key was from a tiger. Second she had been the one in contact with the people at the National Park Service and with Florida Fish and Wildlife through that first process. And last, once the sample had been sent to her museum from the people in Florida, she was the logical one to handle it.

While Shelly was now working in reconstruction, she had really gotten there in sort of a back door way. She had been a double major at Carnegie Mellon in both molecular genetics and art, sculpture being her preferred form. Her family had questioned that second major, but she had pointed out to them that it had no effect on her financial aid and it could have been worse: she could have majored in bagpipes.

While at CMU she had volunteered at the Carnegie Museum in Pittsburgh, helping the people in the dinosaur lab rebuild bones and skeletons and sometimes models of the critters they were from. She had loved that work but knew it wasn't a good career path if she wanted a job, one that would pay well down the road. So she had gotten her graduate degrees in molecular biology and gone to work for one of the pharmaceutical giants in New Jersey.

She made a lot of money, and much of the work was interesting and even exciting at times. But the pressure to get marketable results fast was intense. She found herself working 80 or more hours per week, often at strange hours when experiments needed tending. She had no life and didn't love the atmosphere. She found few friends among her colleagues. When she quit, she wasn't sure what she would do next.

While casting around for a new path, her friend and supervisor at the Carnegie Museum told her about an opening at the Museum of Natural History in New York City for a re-constructor. They loved her background and what they saw of her work. She had been there five years. Now she loved the museum, and she had made loads of friends. Living in a tiny flat in Brooklyn made the city more affordable. Now she had time to enjoy it and people to enjoy it with.

So being the person who had started this whole thing and having the skills in both molecular biology and anatomy made her the logical go-to person. Yuck, she thought.

She had booked some time on the museum's comparison microscope. This is the kind of instrument that lets you see side-by side images of two objects you want to compare. Forensic people use one to compare barrel marks produced on bullets when trying to decide if a bullet came from a particular gun. Shelly was going to use one to compare the hair sample from Florida with hair samples from known animals in the museum's collection. Those samples were well labeled and already mounted for viewing.

She had chosen hair from several known Everglades animals and then some samples from other mammals including tigers.

"Might as well start with the one we called the first round," she said aloud even though she was alone in the room.

When the two images popped up side by side it seemed unlikely that she would have to look any further. They were a fantastic match.

She wanted to be sure but she knew she could be biased from what she concluded before no matter how hard she tried not to be. Shelly called Randy in.

"Have you ever used one of these?" She asked him.

"Yeah, once or twice at school and at another place I interned for a couple of summers," he replied.

"How confident are you that you would be able to find close matches to a sample of hair?" Shelly asked.

"I'm good with that. I took a forensic class for fun last year after my last internship when I had used one of these things. I did well in that part of the lab," Randy said smiling at the bit of bragging he was allowing himself.

"Great," said Shelly. "When you have the time I have a sample here that I'd like you to compare with about a dozen other samples to see if you find one that is a good match."

"I could take time now if you want. I'm between assignments right now and it would be best not to break up my next project once I get it started."

"Super," said Shelly. "Here are the comparison samples. The one to compare them to is already on the scope."

With that Shelly walked out of the lab holding the museum's labeled sample of tiger hair. Let's see if he finds a match in those other samples, she thought.

About an hour or so later Randy knocked on her lab door and stepped in. "I didn't find a thing that was even close in those samples," he said immediately.

Shelly handed him the sample of tiger hair that she had altered by covering over the label so it could not be read. "Here's another one to try. See what you think," she said to him.

Fifteen minutes later he was back with, "That was a dead on match. Care to tell me what that sample was?"

"Tiger," was all she said.

Confirmation would come from the genetics. She had found part of a follicle on the sample. Enough for PCR, a technique that makes many copies of small segments of the genetic material DNA from a sample. Once enough of the DNA is available, it can then be sequenced. Sequencing would tell them the order of the Lego by Lego-like building blocks of the DNA fragment that had been copied. That could then be compared with a huge database to see if there were any matches, hopefully identifying only one species. The technique had been used for years.

The piece of DNA used is from a gene in the cell's powerhouse compartment called a mitochondrion. The gene makes a chemical that allows the cell to trap energy from food. This technique was used so widely and was so definitive that this sequence was considered the "barcode" for each species of organism on the planet whose cells carry mitochondria.

Even though Shelly knew how to do this part of the analysis, the museum usually sent its genetic work out to labs that ran thousands of such samples. Their labs were set up to run these analyses constantly. This made their work fast and consistent. It would take a few days to get the results back.

8

Jake had made it back to his field site in less time than he had anticipated and found the work going smoothly. The park people had promised to call and let him know what they came up with as soon as they knew. It had been a little over a week and he was getting anxious.

Once again his phone rang in his shirt pocket while he was waist deep in water. "These people really know about timing," he said to one of his students.

"This is Jake," he said answering the phone.

"Glad I got you, Jake. This is Steve again from the park. We promised to call when we got more information on that hair sample we found a week or so ago."

"What did you hear?" asked Jake trying not to sound too anxious.

"Definitely tiger. Probably Bengal subspecies."

"Geez man!" exclaimed Jake. "How sure are you?"

"Very. Great match on both hair analysis and DNA they found on a partial follicle."

"You think this is the one that left the print at Lumber Key?"

"Well...." Steve hedged. "This sample was more than 50 miles away from Lumber. That's a lot of swamp to cover. I found a paper from India that tracked some radio-collared tigers in one of their National Parks. None of them had a home range of over 35 miles but this guy is in a very different place. We know Bengals live in swamps but I don't know if one would travel that far. I can't imagine there is more than one out there, though. So probably."

"What's next?" asked Jake.

"We really can't spare enough people to go on a massive search for this thing, so we're thinking we'll set out some motion activated 'camera traps' and some sound activated recording devices and send out alerts to be posted all over the area asking anyone who might spot something to report it to us. Then we'll just wait and see what comes in."

"So what you're saying is that until we get some real positive confirmation it is just sit back and wait," said Jake sounding a bit annoyed.

"I wouldn't say we are going to 'just sit back,'" responded Steve bristling a bit a Jake's attitude. "It's not like we have nothing to do here."

"Yeah, I know," said Jake, embarrassed by his easy anger. "Will you let me know if you find anything more though?"

"Sure. I know you have a very personal interest in the outcome of all this. Talk to you soon."

Patience was not one of Jake's virtues, but wait he must. The whole search for answers was out of his hands now. Jake knew that camera traps and sound recordings had worked well in a number of other situations where monitoring a hard-to-find species was involved, so there was a chance it would yield something in this situation as well. He just wanted it to happen faster than he knew it would.

The good and the bad news was that this whole scenario had flown under the media radar. No one but the current players knew what they were dealing with. Jake had spoken to Al's family, who had asked to be given privacy in their loss. Jake had passed that along to Steve who had honored the family's request. Al's disappearance at Lumber Key had hardly hit any news sources.

If anyone had wanted to alert people to any possible danger from this discovery or if they had wanted the eyes of the general public on the lookout for possible sightings of this probable tiger, they would have had to be a lot more forthcoming with the media than they had been so far. Clearly no one had been thinking along either of those lines.

9

Steve had been a mountain man as a kid. He had grown up in west central Montana and hadn't seen much of the indoors winter or summer in the 24 years he lived there. He had taken his degrees at the university and worked with the bear people on grizzly surveys through his college and grad school days. He had been delighted to get the National Parks job on the first try. He had wanted to stay in the Western Parks but when the job for a good advancement came up in the Everglades he didn't think he could pass it up. He knew he could get back to Montana in the summer to visit family, and Florida had enough appeal for them that he was certain he could entice them there every winter.

He and the other National Park people had worked with Fish and Wildlife before to set out camera traps, mainly for panthers. For this search they decided to deploy three around each of the two sites where a suspicious animal might have been roaming. It was unlikely that an animal would return to a small island like Lumber but they put one out there anyway, along with two more on the closest mainland area. The three at the Shark Valley site were all within about a thousand yards of the observation tower. The traps were motion activated; they recorded digital video for the duration of the motion that tripped them.

Since they had not had experience with sound recording other than what the camera traps could catch, they decided to get long-distance sound recording equipment from the McCauley Library of Natural Sounds at Cornell University's Lab of Ornithology. Researchers there had used those things searching for the "Grail Bird," the thought-to-be-extinct Ivory-Billed Woodpecker, in the swamps of Arkansas. The people at the Lab told them how to deploy, use and maintain the equipment and offered to help in analyzing anything they recorded.

Based on the sparse findings that people from Cornell had gotten with the woodpecker recordings, no one was expecting anything concrete or even suspicious in the near future. Since there were people at Shark Valley every day, Steve suggested that those cameras and sound recorders be checked twice a week. The ones at Lumber would be checked every two weeks if someone could be spared from regular duty to go out there.

A surprise was ahead of them. Ten days after they were deployed, one of the Shark Valley cameras caught something they had hoped wouldn't be there. And the animal that was on that video apparently had discovered and destroyed the other two cameras in the area. The sound equipment caught threatening roars that came along with those actions, and they were spine tingling.

10

"Hey Jake, it's Steve."

This time Jake was in his apartment and not in the swamp when his phone rang.

"What's up, Steve? Got something?"

"You bet. And it's a doozy!"

"Well, don't keep me waiting."

"It's a tiger alright. We got great video of it at the Shark Valley site and really amazing sound recordings too. And get this. The mammal people think it is a female and about 300 pounds … and, based on her swollen belly, possibly pregnant!"

"Pregnant? Does that mean you guys think there is a male out there too?"

"Well, not really. We all think that whoever dropped this baby off probably wanted to get rid of her because she was pregnant and didn't want to deal with that. And besides, the Everglades looked like a good place for her to live and have her cubs."

"Wow. Well what's next?"

"We're going to put out some large animal traps if we can borrow some big enough ones from somewhere and see if we can capture this girl. Then we think this episode will be over."

"Thanks for the call, Steve. Let me know when you've got her. It feels like some closure anyway. Talk to you soon."

Jake let out a sigh and his muscles relaxed with the thought that he now had some real evidence of why Al had disappeared. A tiger dumped in a strange swamp by god knows who would take any food that came its way. Al must have been one of the biggest and easiest prey it had seen since it had been left there. It wasn't pleasant thinking that Al had been taken by a man-eater but at least it was an explanation. It could have just as easily been him that had been taken. Jake would have to cope with that. The search for answers appeared to be over.

11

Whoever leaked the video to the media didn't think about the furor it would cause. Once the tiger was seen by millions on national television and stills were in every print medium in the country, reports came pouring into the park Service and Fish and Wildlife. Most were easy to dismiss. One guy had sent in a picture of his cat in the family swimming pool claiming that he had a tiger in his area too. Another just let out a fake roar when the people set up to take calls answered the phone. Even reports that seemed plausible often were clearly full of holes and guesses when the people calling in were asked for details. It seemed like no credible reports of other sightings were around.

The teams had continued checking the remaining equipment hoping to see this girl again either back at Shark Valley site or, less likely, at the Lumber Key area. Nothing had shown up in the two weeks following the first recorded sightings.

The media blitz prompted something that no one had expected, however. Park rangers and Fish and Wildlife staff began calling in old reports of strange sightings that they had recorded from visitors from well before the disappearance on Lumber Key. Some of these reports were over a year old. Everyone had dismissed them as meaningless at the time. They had to be logged but were never followed up. There were two reports from Nine Mile Pond, four reports from Hell's Bay, three from the Lard Can, and one from the Bay Chickee area, several from the Gulf Coast area around Everglades City, a number from the Big Cypress, and over a dozen from the Flamingo Center. What they all had in common were descriptions that could be linked to an animal as large and as colorful as a tiger but not to any known Everglades mammal. All of these were unlikely to be false since they had come in before the media attention. However many of them were real, it seemed certain that there were more than one or two tigers in the Glades. They all were almost certainly not the same female caught by the camera trap at Shark Valley.

"Flamingo we have a problem," thought Steve after he reviewed all of the reports sent his way. As he sat thinking at his desk, a park ranger walked over and handed him a computer thumb drive.

"You're going to be amazed when you look at what we have here, Steve. This is from the units at Lumber Key. We got good video and good sound recordings just two days ago."

Steve put it in his USB port and ran the video. Sauntering into view was a massive tiger, mouth open and panting. It stared at the camera and stood still briefly, not long enough to shut off the instrument. As it moved slowly off and out of view, it was clear to Steve that he was looking at a male. One much bigger than the female they had seen on the Shark Valley camera.

"Holy shit!" was all he could manage as he stared at the ranger who brought him the drive.

He was beginning to think that maybe Jake's question about the presence of more than one tiger in the Glades was pretty much on the mark. Maybe there were several of these animals out there. And maybe, just maybe, at least two of them had mated.

Steve knew that this would not calm the fuss about a tiger in the Glades that the media had created. It would only inflame it. He felt he had to tell Jake but he decided not to let the information be too widely circulated.

Unfortunately, it already had been.

12

Shelly Lawson was paying more attention to the evening news than she had in a long time. Often it had been just background noise to preparing dinner and getting ready for an evening of reading or channel surfing. Tonight with the report on the tigers in the Everglades, she found herself watching with a much more personal connection.

She and Randy had been right. As strange as it seemed, that pieced-together paw print and the follicle DNA sample had led to the right answer of what was out there in the vast Florida swamp. She decided it was time she learned some more about the Everglades and Florida and tigers.

This night Shelly spent her time on the Internet. She found many references to Marjorie Stoneman Douglass' "River of Grass," the work that best described and defined the Everglades. She had thought that the Glades were just one very large swamp like the ones she passed on her way to her upstate summer vacation spots. Not so. What came through loud and clear in the sites she found was just how much this amazing system of water, grass, hammock, and prairie had been compromised over the years by development in one form or another.

Fresh water had been diverted from the Glades for decades, going to the Gold Coast cities and the farms of central Florida. River flow, both east and west, had been supplemented by Glades water. Exotics had been dumped there by the dozens if not the hundreds, and those that found the place hospitable had taken over and threatened to destroy it completely. In fact it was hard to say it wasn't destroyed already what with the Maleleuca, Brazilian Pepper, and the pythons.

Over a century ago hunters had devastated the bird populations of the Glades for the feathers they provided for women's hats. That practice was stopped largely by the efforts of one Audubon and American Ornithologists Union game warden: Guy Bradley. When he was shot and killed by plume hunters in 1905, his death galvanized the nation to stop killing birds. That led to the revitalization of many populations of badly depleted species. Shelly found that Bradley had even inspired a movie about his efforts, "Wind Across the Everglades," with Burl Ives and Christopher Plummer.

Then alligator hunters had put that creature on the endangered list with profligate killing of the animals for their skin for the fashion industry and for meat. More recently, water depletion again became a massive issue and the Glades were in danger of drying up, changing irreparably. In the last two decades, more exotics started in on the place, compromising even what was left.

Realizations about the Glades' importance to people as well as its animals and plants brought about restrictions on some activities and changes that attempted to soften the insults to the environment. When federal and state governments failed the Glades, citizen volunteers and a few non-profits tried to pick up the slack with mixed success. Even so, it remains a place different from what it was 150 years ago and it continues to be in serious trouble.

Now a new exotic was roaming the place, the tiger. An animal that needed a lot of space and very few people. An animal that could adapt to swamps, forests, even mountains with snow. An animal that now and again fought back and actually killed and ate people. The Glades seemed like as good a place as any for such an animal. Since the native puma, the Florida panther, hadn't fared so well lately, one might expect that tigers would have a tougher time of it. Even if that were the case, apparently some had found a way to survive and maybe even do more than survive—to mate.

Shelly began reading about Florida's efforts to stop the degradation of the Glades. What she read was not encouraging. She was glad to see that there had been a move to create more contiguous natural spaces by establishing a wildlife corridor between the Everglades and the Georgia border. In any wildlife corridor, both ecosystem and gene flow could go in at least two directions. She wasn't convinced that this was good for the Glades but at least it was an acknowledgement that something had to be done.

By the time sleep was ready to take over, Shelly was angry and sad and excited. She had been on the front end of discovering something new in a place that was a treasure. She didn't think what she had found was a good thing, but maybe she had been part of finding it early enough so it wouldn't get out of hand.

13

Florida's Tea Party Governor got word of the tigers in the Glades at the same time as everyone else.

"Ah crap!" he exclaimed as he watched the Fox News report.

He really didn't care a bit about the Glades except as a draw for tourists and a source for water for the Gold Coast and Big Sugar. He did care about his state getting another black eye in the media, however, particularly in a re-election year.

He quickly called his advisors, one of whom claimed to be his environmental guru. He heard that the parks people and Fish and Wildlife were trying to trap the tigers they knew were there and planned to take them to the Big Cat Rescue place in Tampa, whatever that was. He really just wished they would quietly kill the suckers and stop this nonsense in its tracks.

His PR people said they could manage the publicity from here on out and minimize the fallout about another man-eater in Florida. They hadn't done such a good job over the last four years about sharks and shark attacks, particularly on the East coast, and the latest bear attack in Lakeland, but he had to trust somebody to manage the message.

One advisor made a suggestion that startled everyone. He thought the tigers could be used to entice people to Florida on tours to see them "in the wild". He joked that maybe they could get some Indian or Sri Lankan to run elephant safaris into the glades for these tiger hunts (photo shoots).

That set off more ideas. One guy proposed actually selling rights to hunt the tigers for real and killing them. The hunter could keep the head for mounting and the state could sell the skins and the carcasses to Thailand or someplace like that for "traditional medicine." No telling how much money they could make from that.

The problem with all of these ideas was that the tigers were in a National Park and under federal protection. The governor was sure he could arrange to get around that problem if only they could come up with a single consistent strategy.

By the time the meeting was over, it was obvious that no decisions would be made until more was known about how big this problem was. The only hope for the short term was to get the stories out of the news as fast as possible. That wouldn't be so easy.

14

"Hi Steve, its Jake. I haven't heard anything in a couple of weeks and I'm wondering how you're coming on the tiger trapping."

"Good to hear from you Jake. We had to get some bigger traps shipped down to us from up north, culvert traps for bears. We looked into other things but we just don't have the man-power for net or cage drop traps and we certainly can't try tranquilizer dart hunting since we can't seem to find the animals very easily anyway.

"We put the culvert traps out and baited them with horse meat. Not even a glimmer based on the motion detection cams we have out there. Actually we did have some glimmers, but they turned out to be possums and raccoons. No tiger."

"How long do you plan to give it?"

"We're thinking about three weeks, Jake. If we don't get something by the end of that time, we'll have to re-think how to go about this. We really aren't very hopeful. Culvert traps haven't been used for tigers as far as we know, so we're flying blind here."

"Any chance I could be of some help? I have a month or so before classes start and we have most of the data from my field sites, so I could do analysis and writing while I was out there with you folks."

"We'd love to have you, but I'm not sure what we'd have you do right now. It's just wait and see at the moment. Give us some time and let's find out if this is going to work."

"OK, Steve. Anything else you can tell me about this tiger business?"

"We've interviewed all the rangers who took in the reports of sightings all over the Glades."

"And…?"

"Most all had pretty much the same story. People reported seeing something that they thought was big, orangish, and cat-like. Only one claimed what they saw was a tiger. This was down near Flamingo on one of the dry trails."

"Did they get a picture on a cell phone or something?"

"No, but the report claims the animal showed no fear and walked up to them on the trail as if it wanted to say hello. Obviously, the ranger who took the report said he had a hard time not laughing in their faces."

"What do you think of that report now?"

"Well, it could have happened. If the animal was a tiger and had been a pet before it was dropped in the Glades, it might actually be looking for people to feed it and take it back home."

"A pet!?"

"Yeah, a pet. You wouldn't believe what people keep as pets."

"Aren't tigers a protected species?"

"They are but there is an illicit pet trade in all sorts of exotic animals, even endangered ones."

"Do you think that encounter actually happened?"

"Once the ranger knew about our tiger pictures, he wasn't laughing anymore."

"Anyone down there in the Flamingo area looking for that animal?"

"Not really. We still have no idea whether we're looking for two animals or more so we aren't going to spread ourselves thin on wild-tiger chasing."

"What if I came down and camped at Flamingo for a while and looked for the animal or more evidence from there?"

"It could be helpful if you really want to, and I do know you have a vested interest. I could set it up so that you have the use of a campsite free for as long as you want. I would recommend that you don't go out alone, though. Even in developed areas like that, you never know what you'll run into."

"OK, Steve. I'll see if I can persuade one of my students to come down with me for a while before classes start. How about we shoot for this coming Sunday for me to get there? I think I can wrap things up and be there by then.

"By the way, is there Wi-Fi and phone reception there?"

"Oh yeah. Good on both accounts. I'll set it up with the office people there. Let me know when you are set to go out. I'll let you know more about where to start."

"Great, Steve. You'll hear from me in a few days."

15

Years ago, Jake had decided that camping didn't mean living like a barbarian. He had a fairly large travel trailer with air conditioning and heat. It had its own generator for maximum independence. It could be hooked up to water and even sewage. It easily slept four but he rarely took anyone with him when he went anywhere in it. He just didn't want to tent camp these days unless he was backpacking, and he hated motels.

He drove past the visitor center, along Flamingo Way. Just past Eco pond, he pulled into the T Loop of Flamingo campground and found his site. The sites are mostly open grassy ground with picnic tables and grills. He had a canoe on top and a couple of bikes on a rack at the back.

It wasn't long before he had the truck unhooked and the camper ready to go. He and his student Mike sat in the shade and sipped a beer once they were set up. Mike was a senior and probably headed to grad school at the end of this year. He was a good field worker and he had been quick to volunteer when Jake explained what they were going to do for the next few weeks. Jake had left his other students plenty to do back in the lab.

Steve had gotten Jake a campsite near the visitor center so they could take advantage of all the amenities and information there. He had also arranged for Jake to stay in the same campsite for as long as he wanted rather than having to move sites every two weeks to comply with National Park regulations.

"How 'bout we take a walk partway along the Coastal Prairie Trail and then back near the water?" Jake asked.

"Let's do it!"

Jake had to wonder if Mike's enthusiasm would last in the heat and humidity, although he had spent long hot days on Jake's study sites.

Jake strapped on the Smith and Wesson M29 .44 magnum he had gotten permission to bring with him on this venture in case they needed it when they ran into one of the tigers. It was an original old revolver his dad had bought years ago, thinking he would do some varmint hunting with it. It had been used only a few times for target practice, though, before his dad died and it passed on to Jake. It had a kick that could break an arm and an explosive sound to match. He wasn't certain that even this cannon-like handgun would have enough stopping power for a big cat but he was damn certain that the usual 9 mm service sidearm most officials carried would have the effect of a mosquito bite on one of those big critters. The .44 was reported to be able to bring down elk or even Cape buffalo when it was first advertised. Guns had been allowed in most National Park camping areas since 2009 but not carried openly as he was about to do. Steve had arranged everything for him, including this. He wondered about anyone else still in the park without a weapon, though, since the park service had not closed the place or limited access to any area.

It was late in the day so the temperature was beginning to moderate. There were very few people in the campsite and no one on the trail. The whole walk was as quiet as anything either man had experienced in quite some time. No sounds but a slight wind in the pines, a few animal rustlings and their footsteps on the trail.

They were on edge the whole time, looking for any sign out of the ordinary. By the time they were ready to head back, the sun had dipped low in the sky and was no longer a hammer slamming into the earth with its heat. The walk back was easy but uneventful.

Mike set up the camp stove and fired up the grill. Steaks, fried potatoes and salad were soon on the plates and ready to eat. A few beers would be part of this meal as well. Good nutrition there, Mike thought.

As they sat watching the sky darken and the stars come out, a low rumbling roar sounded from back up the trail they had just hiked. It didn't sound too far away.

"Probably a bull alligator," said Jake. "Let's see if we can record it if it roars again and check it with the ranger in the morning."

They both turned on their cell phones to record. The roar was repeated twice more, once from where they first heard it and once from further away. The animal was probably moving away from them fast.

By the third post-dinner beer Jake and Mike had had the course and headed into the cool of the camper. They dropped off to sleep almost as soon as they got horizontal.

16

"Mind if we play you something we recorded last night from our camp site?" Jake asked the ranger at the front desk of the visitor center the next morning.

"Go to it," she replied. "I've got nothing but time until someone comes in needing something."

Jake and Mike took turns playing back what they had recorded.

"That's not a gator," said the ranger. "It's not a panther either. I don't have any idea what that is. I've never heard anything like that before around here. Are both those sounds from the same animal?"

"As far as we know. We never saw the animal or any evidence of what it was."

"The guys up at Shark valley seem to be more on this than we are down here. Why don't you send that up to them and see what they think. It might be your tiger or who knows what? While you're waiting to hear back you could always go out and try to find some physical evidence of what was out there. You need anything from us here to do that?"

"No, we're good. We have bikes, a canoe, swamp gear and all kinds of sampling equipment. I'll get back to you if we find we need anything else. Thanks."

"Good hunting. And don't tell anyone I phrased it that way, please."

"No worries," said Jake, ushering Mike out the door.

17

"I thought this had gone away," growled the Governor. "How'd the papers get hold of this stuff?"

"Some guys down in the Glades recorded some sounds on their cell phones and the park service sent them up to Cornell to find out what made them. Up there they tracked it down to tiger, and whoever did the tracking also found out that it was more than one animal making the sounds. Apparently they had some pictures and sounds from some other area down there that screamed tiger, too," replied an aide.

"Well hell, I can read. That's what the papers say. What I want to know is how did it get to the media in the first place and how come they decided to make it such a big story? I want this gone ASAP."

"We have no idea how this got out. There are so many moving parts in this situation there could be any number of players who could be telling what they know. As far as the media are concerned, how would we know why they chose to play something like this up? Maybe the wars in the Middle East and the genocides in Africa and Asia aren't selling enough ads."

"Well figure it out and get it fixed. That's what you're paid for. No excuses. This is going to cost us one way or another."

"I'll do my best, sir."

"Your best better be having it gone. Have the national people talked about closing the park or limiting access to some areas or anything like that? It could make us have to think about some closings too."

"Not that I've heard, sir."

"God, you're just a vacuum of information today aren't you? Get on it, son. I want answers and I want results NOW! Get gone and don't let the door hit you in the ass on the way out."

"Yes sir," said the aide rushing into the hall.

18

Shelly looked down at the glycine envelopes on the bench in front of her and just shook her head.

"Why the hell would anybody be so careless collecting samples like this," she wondered silently. The hair, vegetation and soil samples that had been sent to her were useless for any molecular work. The envelopes weren't sealed properly, had finger prints on them which meant they were handled without gloves, and hadn't been separated so there could be no cross-contamination. In short, they were a mess. She could do some more microscope work on the hair but it probably wouldn't tell her even as much as the first sample she had been sent. That first sample had been collected and preserved the way it should have been. Clearly the people who took these samples didn't really know what they were doing.

Shelly passed the hair sample to Randy. "I have no idea why they keep sending this material to us. Surely there have to be people down there in at least some of those universities that can handle this kind of analysis."

"It's kind of fun to be involved, though, don't you think?"

"Well yes, it is, to be honest. Anyway, see what you can do with this on the comparison microscope. Don't worry about contaminating anything though. They really botched the collecting. We can't do any PCR or any real chemical analysis on these samples. There is just too much room for contamination here."

"Got it. Shouldn't take long. Where did all this come from by the way?"

"Remember me telling you about this guy from some Gulf Coast place who called me and got angry about all this?"

"Yes I do. And by the way, it's Florida Gulf Coast University down in Ft. Meyers and they made it to the Sweet Sixteen in NCAA basketball not long ago and weren't even expected to make the tournament."

"I guess I should be impressed but basketball ain't molecular biology."

"OK. Just thought you'd like to know."

"I'll be sure to wear my best sports bra if I ever meet this guy. Anyway, he and a student of his are down in the Glades now trying to find more evidence of what is out there. They collected these samples. He's a field biologist and ecology guy who hasn't seemed to catch on to the idea that even in that field he's got to know how to get and use molecular data in the 21st century."

As Randy walked out the door, Shelly's department head came in and sat on one of the lab stools beside her bench.

"Just got a call from the National Park people. They would like to have you go down to the Everglades and work with them on this tiger issue. They liked the thoroughness and detail of your analysis of those last samples and want to make sure they do any more of that kind of sampling right."

"I've just been talking to Randy and saying that I really don't know why they don't use people who are already down there? Why me? There have to be really good people all over Florida."

"Hey, I'm just conveying a message here. I have no idea why they want you rather than more local people. Maybe it's just they want to go with a known quantity with excellent quality rather than take a crap shoot with someone else. What I do see is that this is an opportunity for the museum to get some really positive press. Having them come to us makes good copy."

"I really don't want to go. I've got a lot going on here."

"I know your projects, Shelly. There's nothing here that can't be put on hold for a time. This really could be good for the museum."

Shelly paused to let it sink in that her department head wasn't really asking her but telling her to go.

"If I have to go, I'd really like to find some way to get Randy there too. He's more excited about this project than I am and he's been a big help with those samples and analyses. I know he's just an intern but he's with us through December so he could be reassigned."

"Let me look into that. I expect we can find a way. The National Park Service and Florida Fish and Wildlife will fund you while you're there but only for so much. We'll pick up the rest as we can. It'll be contract work. We've got be careful with the budget."

"Get back to me on the details and Randy's involvement and I'll feel a lot better about saying yes then," Shelly said, knowing that there was only one possible answer she could give, no matter what.

"OK, Shelly. I should be back with you later today."

The first thing Shelly did was check the weather in the Glades. Ninety-five degrees and 74 percent humidity with afternoon thunderstorms and high winds. Tropical summer in the middle of hurricane season. Just the time to be in South Florida. Brooklyn seemed even better than it did yesterday.

19

Shelly and Randy were met at the Ft. Lauderdale airport by a woman in a National Park ranger uniform. Shelly was glad to see that she had the good sense to leave her silly Smokey Bear hat in the car before coming to baggage claim.

Randy had talked Shelly through what to pack in case they were deployed to the field, a fate Shelly was hoping wouldn't be necessary. With all of that, some sampling equipment, and her "regular" travel gear, she had more baggage for this trip than any she had taken anywhere in her life. Just getting to this airport was more of a hassle than she really wanted.

As they stepped out of the air conditioning, they were greeted by the sodden heat of a late morning mid-summer South Florida day. Shelly felt like she was having trouble breathing as she schlepped all her gear to the van in the parking garage. Randy didn't seem to notice either the heat or the inconvenience of having so much baggage to deal with.

They learned from the ranger that they were driving south to Flamingo where the park Service had a visitor's RV parked at the camp ground. So much for not being deployed to the field. It was supposedly big enough to accommodate both Shelly and Randy and allow privacy. These certainly weren't the conditions Shelly would have preferred. Sharing living space with a male intern seemed like a giant step back to college living, something she had told herself she would never tolerate again. Clearly she was no fan of "Big Brother" TV shows.

She tried to relax as much as possible once they were on the road, but the traffic and the crazy driving patterns started taking their toll on her nerves even before they were past the Miami exits on I 95. Somehow the chaos of NYC seemed very sane by comparison.

The time it had taken for the AC to kick in once they started driving seemed interminable. Now she was just dripping wet with cold air blasting on her face.

"So, do you have any lab facilities down where we're going?" she asked the ranger.

"Not really. There are some microscopes and some old chemicals and glassware around, but mostly just field gear and computers."

"We'll need for someone to organize getting a lot of equipment and chemicals down there so we can set up a lab."

"I guess you'll have to talk to the director about where to get what you want and whether we can spare any space for you."

"Great," thought Shelly. "And I thought only museums and arts organizations ran on a shoestring with no resources." She had assumed her department head had cleared all that with the park people before they left. So much for assumptions. She should have guessed as much when she heard about the RV.

They pulled into what looked like a gas station near Homestead. It bordered a stagnant creek lined with sub-tropical scrubby vegetation. To one side of the main building was clearly a fishing store, bait shop and small fishing boat rental place. There were metal tanks under the eaves marked "Live Bait." The parking lot was filled with pickups.

"Time for some lunch," said the ranger.

Randy was smiling like a kid. This was all new for him. He had been born raised and gone to school in inland Maine and had never been to Florida. His family just didn't have the means to make the Florida theme park pilgrimages that so many of the kids he grew up with seemed to make every spring break.

"Lunch?" thought Shelly. "I don't eat live bait!"

The restaurant was a 1950s fluorescent-lit, Formica-tabled affair. Almost every table was filled with people. To Shelly's surprise it seemed to be mostly families and mostly black and Hispanic. The men had taken off their big straw hats and laid long machetes beside their chairs. Everyone was smiling and talking animatedly both to their families and to everyone else it seemed. They sat down at the only empty table.

A waitress from an "I Love Lucy" episode strode over to their table.

"What'll y'all have ta drink."

"Iced tea with lemon," said the ranger. Shelly and Randy indicated the same.

When she came back with the tea, Shelly couldn't wait to drink it down. She was really thirsty from the drive. It was so sweet she almost gagged. Randy made a face but didn't react nearly as strongly to the flavor.

"Sorry," said the ranger. "I should have told you that all tea is sweet down here unless you say differently."

The waitress didn't seem to even notice as she took out her pad and said, "Let's start with you, honey," referring to Shelly. "What'll you have?"

"I haven't looked at a menu."

"Well there ain't but a few choices and they're up there on the wall. I'll come back to you then. All of 'em come with coleslaw and fries or mac 'n cheese."

"Do you have salads or fruit?"

"Y'all ain't from around here, are ya?"

"No, not really," Shelly replied sheepishly.

When they got their food and tucked in Shelly was surprised at how fresh and tasty it all was. Simple and abundant and very good. Randy ate enthusiastically and polished off what Shelly couldn't finish.

Shelly and Randy learned later that many of the families in the place were cane workers from the "Big Sugar" fields in the surrounding counties.

When they climbed back into the van, it had once again become an oven. "They better have turned on the AC in that RV we are going to or there will be hell to pay from me," thought Shelly. She was asleep by the time they made the turn into the park.

20

Miccosukee tribe members had been running airboat tours of the Glades for decades. Bobby Oakleaf ran an operation called *Tiger Gators Airboats* about half way across the Glades off the Tamiami Trail. His business was very slow in the summer with all the heat. When he read about the tigers in the Glades he jumped at the chance to capitalize on the news and gain the upper hand because of his fortuitous company name.

He advertised "Tiger Safaris" far and wide on both coasts. He figured that people would travel at least two hours for a two-hour safari. He doubled his usual price and carefully worded his messages so there was no guarantee of actually seeing a tiger.

Less than 48 hours after he had posted his online ads and asked the tribal casino and resort to run his ads on their continuous-play video screens, he had a bunch of bookings for the tiger tours.

The first group to arrive shouldn't have been driving. They were a mixed group of young Europeans who had been at the casino drinking while they lost their money. They were noisy and blitzed. He almost turned them away but then thought the better of it.

Everyone piled into the boat and put on the padded earphones to muffle the engine noise. They listened to Captain Bobby's hokey patter and even talked to each other over the noise.

The good captain set a slow speed and headed into the closest wide-open slough. The breeze made the late morning heat almost pleasant. While the sawgrass was high and seemed to go on forever, Bobby was still able to show those passengers who were able to focus egrets, herons, moorhens, alligators and a couple of raccoons.

About an hour into the ride Bobby spotted something big running through the water and grass to his right and seeming to come at just the right angle to run into them. He'd never seen anything do that before. If anything, animals would run away from the boat. He had a hard time telling just what it was that he was seeing.

Bobby slowed the boat and several people claimed they also saw something in the grass. To give the animal a chance to go by without incident Bobby stopped the boat. The animal seemed to change course again, angling straight toward the boat. Several people were now on their none-too-steady feet.

Suddenly a large orange and black animal burst out of the grass headed at the boat. It was clearly a tiger.

Several of the passengers were not too drunk to have their cellphones and cameras rolling to capture what they were seeing. The animal roared as it lunged at the boat.

Bobby hammered the throttle home and turned the wheel away from the oncoming tiger. Two people who had been standing were thrown from the boat and into the water as it lurched away from the leaping animal. They landed in the water directly in the path of the animal.

Bobby slowed the boat when it was out of range of the lunging tiger. Everyone watched in disbelief as the large animal quickly dispatched both people in the water before they could even stand or scream. The tiger gave a deafening roar, picked up the body of the nearest dead tourist in its mouth and headed back into the sawgrass toward a nearby hammock.

The panic on the boat was immediate. Bobby screamed for everyone to sit down but two more drunken people had already jumped into the water and were heading to the remaining bleeding body in the water. Cameras were on.

Bobby swung the boat around and idled over to the tourists who were trying through their alcoholic miasma to determine if there were still any signs of life. None appeared. Bobby kept scanning the area where the tiger had disappeared with the other body hoping to see no more movement in their direction.

With more sobriety than Bobby thought possible from this group, several people helped lift the body onto the boat, covered it in shirts quickly stripped off several of the men, and the tourists in the swamp climbed back into the boat.

"Holy shit, so much for my airboat business," thought Bobby. He had no doubt that some of the pictures and videos taken of this incident as well as a bunch of stories would be hitting the press very soon. But first he had to get rid of these people and report the incident to the park people, the police and the tribe. Most importantly he had to get this body taken care of. It was going to be a very long couple of days.

21

"Is there some kind of unpublished dress code for field biologists, or did you learn how to dress like that in high school?" was the first thing Shelly said when she saw Jake for the first time as they met in the campground the next morning. Mike and Randy came close to laughing out loud at that question. In fact, Mike did lose a little coffee through his nose.

Jake was standing outside his camper in his usual long-sleeve safari shirt, long cargo pants, jungle boots and canvas mesh

Australian drover hat. He had come down to greet Shelly and Randy as they came over to his camper after breakfast. Shelly stood there in shorts, sandals and a tank top.

While taken aback a bit by the sarcastic comment, Jake did manage a smile.

"I give you about ten minutes out here in that getup before you understand the wisdom of my sartorial choices."

"We'll see."

Shelly had practically bathed in 100% Deet before exiting her RV. Even so, she was beginning to notice that the insect population in the campground didn't seem to give a rip about Deet.

"So, let me introduce myself. I'm Jake Ballard. I was with the guy who got taken off Lumber Key. And this guy is Mike Aronson, a student of mine at Gulf Coast. He's here for a while before he heads back to classes. I'm here until we get some resolution on this tiger business. I'm taking a leave for the rest of the summer and fall."

"Good to meet you," Shelly replied with more enthusiasm than she was actually feeling.

"I'm Shelly Lawson, AKA the 're-constructor' by museum geeks. This is Randy Benoit. He's an intern in our department. Randy was the first to i.d. the tiger print in that Rorschach mess they sent us from the island search."

Handshakes all around eased the transition to camp chairs around a fire ring Steve had gotten permission for them to set up in spite of the park rules that no fires outside of grills were allowed. Mike took coffee and tea orders and went back into Jake's camper to get everyone something to hold while they talked.

"What have you all learned about these tigers since you've been here, Dr. Ballard?"

"Please, everyone just call me Jake."

"OK, Jake?"

"Not much. We recorded a couple of roars and checked them out with the sound library people at Cornell. They're saying that we had two different animals on the recordings. If that's true, we know we have more tigers around than anyone thought at the beginning, but no one is speculating on just how many might be out there."

"Are they all the same subspecies?" Randy asked.

"You'd know that better than we would. You guys have been sent any DNA samples that have been collected."

"Yeah, why have we gotten all those samples and not had them sent to some of the labs down here?" Shelly asked.

"The parks people wanted consistency. You had been in on this from the beginning and had done a hell of a good job. They thought they'd stick with a quality known."

"Thanks." Shelly and Randy both couldn't help a little smile with this unexpected compliment.

"We do have to talk about DNA and molecular sampling in general," said Shelly. "Everything but the first envelope with the hair sample came to us too contaminated to do any work on. We need to get some sterile protocols going on this project and whoever is out there doing the collecting better trained up."

"Sorry about that." Jake was trying very hard not to show just how annoyed he was with this woman. "I know you said the first sample was the Bengal subspecies. What other possibilities are there?"

"Randy?" said Shelly deferring to him.

"There are four other subspecies that might be there, the Indochinese, the Malayan, the South-China, and the Sumatran. There is another subspecies, but it isn't too likely to be here since it is adapted to cold weather, snow and mountains. That's the Siberian."

"We won't know if any of these are part of the group out there until we get samples we can really test," Shelly explained.

By now Mike was back with coffee all around, but Shelly was starting to swat at the swarms that had found her.

"I think I'm beginning to see why you're in long clothes," Shelly said waving away whatever was buzzing in her left ear. "But you have got to have air conditioning units in those clothes to stand this heat and humidity."

"Not really," said Mike. "We just ignore it and we stopped caring about sweat marks years ago."

"Well you boys carry on out here. I'm headed in. If you care to join me I brought some bagels, lox and cream cheese from Brooklyn and we can continue this in more comfort."

The three guys watched Shelly move quickly, trying not to look like she was running, back to her RV.

"What do you think?" Jake asked as Shelly disappeared inside.

"I just finished breakfast but I can always eat," Mike replied.

"You won't be sorry about that decision," said Randy, knowing where Shelly had gotten her bagels and lox.

They slowly made their way across the campground, cups still in hand.

22

"Steve Hamilton," said Steve by way of introduction to the four in the campground. He had come down to Flamingo for a meeting with the park administrators who would decide next steps in following up on the tiger sightings.

"Thanks for being here and for all the work you've put into this already, guys. The meeting is going to start in a few minutes. We'd like all four of you to join us in case there are things you can add to the discussion. I hate to mention it, but please remember that any decisions we come to today are the park's to make. Let's do it."

They headed into Park Headquarters and gathered in the meeting room. Hard to believe they had Styrofoam cups for the coffee and tea, but there they were.

After being introduced all around and gotten their drinks, everyone sat down and got ready for business.

Steve started it off. "The agenda I put in front of you should take us through where we are with the tiger sightings in the park and give us enough of a starting point to possibly make some decisions about where we need to go from here. I'm sure you all remember that this started back in May with the disappearance of Al Jordan, Jake's friend, up in the Ten Thousand Islands."

"The only thing we got there was something like a partial animal print which we sent out for analysis. Shelly Lawson here and Randy Benoit worked that up and came back saying it was a tiger paw print. No one believed it."

"Neither did we," thought Shelly.

"Then we had another sighting by a tourist at Shark Valley. From the search there we got a sample and again sent it up to Shelly and Randy. That came back with a positive DNA for Bengal tiger."

One of the other administrators in the room asked if they were sure it was a Bengal tiger and what other kinds of tigers were possible. Shelly deferred to Randy for the answers.

"That led us to look at old reports from park visitors that were never considered reasonable until we got back these results. The slide I have up on the screen there lists those reports that we have on hand. There might be more that weren't written up, but these are the ones that were documented."

Up on the screen were almost 30 incident reports from all over the park over the last 18 months. All were reports from park visitors. Not one was from a ranger or even a volunteer. There were two reports from Youth Conservation Corps seasonals but these were the least detailed of any of the reports.

"One question I have is why we don't have possible sightings from our own people if there actually are tigers out there?" asked one of the more senior people in the room.

"What do you think would happen to a ranger or other park employee who claimed to see a tiger in the park?" asked one of the rangers in the room. "Think a Bigfoot sighting in the Smokies."

"Yeah, OK."

"All of the sightings were shelved and dismissed as nonsense until now. They all were in sawgrass or dense hammocks. No pictures of any kind until…." Steve paused and then switched the image on the screen to the video they had from the camera traps they had out.

Almost a collective "Jesus!" filled the room as the tiger walked into the picture.

"Now Jake and Mike have some sound recordings and the people at Cornell claim they are from two different animals. It's beginning to look like 'Houston, We have a problem!'"

"How many animals are out there?" asked one participant.

"We have no idea. It is certainly more than one and it could be dozens. That's what these folks are here to help find out," said Steve referring to Shelly, Mike, Randy and Jake.

"Should we be thinking about closing the park until we get this resolved?" asked one of the regional heads.

"We could, but when you think that we have other parks with dangerous animals like grizzlies and cougars, and even the possibility of jaguars in the Southwest, and we don't close those parks even when there is an attack or even a death, I don't see it happening here," said the park director.

"Why are these animals here?" asked another attendee.

"Think pythons," Randy said. "People who kept them as pets found they got too big or started to get aggressive or ate too much or, or, or … No zoo or shelter would take them even if these folks had them legally because most zoos and sanctuaries are at or over capacity and funding is shrinking. So they just dumped them in the nearest habitat that seemed appropriate. It just so happened that the Glades is a wonderful habitat for pythons, and they started finding each other, mating, and eating everything they could get their coils around."

"Sure, but tigers aren't just kept as pets everywhere, right?"

"I can shed some light on that," Randy said. "I did some background on this, and if it's OK with Steve, I can share some of what I came up with."

"Go for it, Randy. That's what we're here for."

"Right now there are about 5000 tigers listed with the USDA."

"The USDA?" someone asked in surprise.

"Yes the USDA. They are charged with inspecting shelters, holding stations, rescue organizations and individuals with permits for big cats. I can't tell you why them, though. If I can use your computer, Steve?" Randy asked pulling out a memory stick.

Steve nodded and Randy plugged in and brought up a small map of the US with red flags all over it.

"This is an interactive map I found through a website for Big Cat Rescue in Tampa. Each of the flags here shows where there are tigers, how many there are at each site, and when they were last inspected. The numbers represent how many were there when they were inspected, and how many are suspected to be there now. You'll notice that a lot of the ones I click on show a reduction in numbers from their inspection date 'til now."

"A lot of the ones you just clicked on seem to be labeled 'sanctuaries.' Isn't that a good thing?" asked the super.

"Not always. They may pass muster for housing the animals minimally but really are just backyard zoos or roadside attractions to get families to stop and buy all sorts of things. Let me show you some others here, too."

Randy clicked on some of the flags on the map. Flag after flag brought up the name of an individual who owned one or more tigers. These were not organizations. Their addresses suggested homes and even some urban apartments where they were kept. Looks of astonishment at the sheer numbers they were looking at were on everyone's face.

"These are the licensed ones," Randy continued. "You can probably expect to even double this number when you take into account all the illegal trade in exotic pets that goes on."

"There are only a few of those flags in South Florida though," observed Jake. "That probably means there aren't that many that could have been dumped out here."

"You might assume that if I hadn't run across some of these postings on a variety of social media," said Randy, flashing up and scrolling through an extensive list of postings from about a half a dozen social media sites.

"These were posted by and directed specifically at illegal pet owners and even more specifically at ones who own tigers. They set up a chain of communication with the code name 'Frosted Flakes.' Think Tony the Tiger on that. Lots of chatter recommending everyone who can to get down here to drop their unwanted animals in the Glades because it is such good habitat for them and they will survive here. It seems tiger owners want to give their animals a good life even if they can't keep them.

These messages go back at least two years and probably more. That means anyone anywhere in the US who could get their tiger here could have left it here. We might be talking about dozens, maybe more."

Shelly looked on, very proud of Randy's work and his professionalism, and even more delighted that she had insisted on his coming along on this project.

At that juncture a knock came on the meeting room door. The administrative assistant opened it. Several of the group near the door were about to tell him they were in the middle of something and to wait when he said, "Sorry to interrupt but this can't wait. We just got a report from up north that two tourists were killed in a tiger attack in the Glades on a Miccosukee airboat tour. One of them wasn't recovered. There is pretty general panic up there. Two of the other tourists got pictures and video. Everyone is assuming that this will hit the media sometime today. Thought you'd want to know."

"Ah shit no!" said the park director, reflecting everyone's reaction. This would change the rest of this discussion.

23

"What the hell do you mean they closed the park until further notice?" screamed the governor. "Do you know what that is going to do to our economy down there? Do you know how that's going to look in all the promotions about coming to Florida for the winter? If they're going to do that the least they could do is let us go in there and drain the place and sell some of it off for development like they should have let us do a century ago! Who the hell are these cretins?"

"Uh. The National Park Service," replied his aide. "And you should know that Florida Fish and Wildlife is supporting them in this too. Not only that, Audubon has closed Corkscrew until there is some assessment of where these animals are and how many are out there."

"You mean to tell me they don't even know how many tigers are in the Glades?"

"Yes sir. That's the case."

"No matter how many are out there, you don't just go closing up a major tourist draw for an entire state because some Germans turn out to be lunch. Hell, even Sea World didn't shut down everything when that Shamu fish ate a trainer. They kept it open, ran damage control, and kept the cash flowing."

"Maybe we could position it as keeping Florida safe for everyone while they enjoy the beaches and the sun."

"Yeah and what are we going to say about the dozen or more shark bites that happen here every year even though it's been a few years since someone died? They don't close the beaches for those."

"Uh, not all, but yes they do locally. They seem to be doing the same kind of thing with the Glades, sir. I think we ought to ask the State Parks people to close at least Collier-Seminole and Fakahatchee Strand since they're so tied to the Glades through Big Cypress. They might even suggest others to close too."

"How soon will the National Park reopen? How can we minimize the fallout from this? How many goddamn tigers are out there and when will we know? And why do you continue to have no answers for me, buddy boy? One more try. Get this buried now!"

"I'm on it," said the aide, backing out the door.

"Like a wart on a sunburned nose," the governor mumbled to himself.

24

"The gold standard for tiger population estimation is capture-recapture assessments. That's been used in India for decades. Most tigers live in areas that are hard to survey and that makes physical trapping almost impossible, so they use camera trap capture and stripe matching to do that."

Steve had done the homework before the meeting at Flamingo and was ready with an idea of how to find out just how many tigers were in the Glades. The need to know was even more urgent now.

"We just can't get enough camera traps or manpower to analyze the images from them to cover an area the size we're working with here in the park. We're open to ideas."

"What about using volunteers from all over South Florida? Could be a citizen science kind of thing," suggested the park super.

"Can we really use 'citizens' since we closed the park to the public until further notice for safety reasons?" Steve asked.

"Good point, Steve."

"I found a couple of articles from India that said fecal DNA analysis of field samples and paw print matching could be used for estimating tiger populations in their national parks," added Shelly.

"They use mitochondrial DNA for tiger i.d. and what they call microsatellites for individual animal i.d.," added Randy.

"We probably have a problem with each of these techniques," Jake interjected. "Remember this is a big wetland and these animals are pooping in the water where no feces remain intact. We also had one heck of a time figuring out that first paw print on Lumber Key because it was under water. This won't be very straightforward."

"On the DNA front we can i.d. tiger DNA in water samples even if there are no visible feces in the water. We have very specific primers for PCR for a whole range of species, including tiger. Primers are short sequences of RNA that start the process of DNA replication binding to an open strand of the double stranded DNA and calling in enzymes that match up the building blocks to make new strands. You can get them very species-specific. If there is enough DNA there we can even i.d. individuals and get a sense of how many different animals contributed to the DNA in each sample, too," Shelly pointed out.

"A while back the guy who won the race to sequence the human genome decided to try to find out how many species of organism were in the ocean. He had *beaucoup* bucks by then and a big yacht. He tooled around the South Pacific collecting water samples and doing DNA analysis. He came up with some startling estimates of species diversity that we had no idea about. His water samples were as clear as the water in your Styrofoam cups, but he got good data. We can do the same here with tigers," Shelly said with more confidence than she actually felt.

"We won't likely get many paw prints but we can certainly look. What we need most is manpower for the fieldwork," Steve said.

"I can put in a request to have some personnel from other National Parks assigned to us for a while. I'll also ask Fish and Wildlife and maybe the Nature Conservancy and Audubon to give us some of their trained field people for this work. How many do you think we will need?" asked the super.

"Let me get together with some other park and Conservancy scientists and we'll get back to you ASAP with an estimate of how many people it will take and a preliminary plan of attack," Steve replied.

"OK if Mike and I sit in on those conversations?" Jake asked.

"Mike, actually I think we have to get you out of the park. You are still a student. I don't think we want to bend the rules for park closure on this one. Only paid professionals this time. Too dangerous," replied Steve. "You can sit in though, Jake."

"We can start to work on what we need in order to do the DNA and paw print analysis for any samples that come our way, and Shelly can work up a training protocol for sample collection," Randy added.

"We can even do the sample collection training over Skype if you want," said Shelly. "It would speed things up getting people into the field from the more distant sites."

"All well and good," said the super. "But we also need to arm the teams so we don't lose anyone out there while we're looking. Can't be the little 9mms we usually have around either. I'll track down some better weapons for the teams while you all are on the rest. Talk to you tonight."

It was lunchtime but no one who was in the room felt the need for food just then, not even Mike.

25

"I'm sorry I brought you all the way down here just to have you go home in a few days," Jake said to Mike.

"Hey, I understand. I don't like it but I do understand. The only question now is how I'm getting home. I came down in your truck."

"If you don't mind my driving your truck," said Randy, "I can take Mike up to Miami and he can fly back to Ft. Myers. That way Shelly can be here to start work on DNA and print recognition set ups and you could be here to talk to the other field people with Steve. I could pick up another load of good groceries while I'm up there, too."

"OK with you, Mike?" asked Jake.

"As if I have a choice, right?"

"OK, Randy. Here are the keys. Should be plenty of gas. While you guys make your way I'll call ahead and get you the earliest flight I can, Mike. I'll pay for everything so don't worry. Can you get home from the airport when you get back?"

"Sure, no problem there."

"Let's get on the road, Mike," said Randy heading for the truck.

"How about giving me 10 minutes to pack up my gear, OK?"

"Oh, sorry. Sure thing."

Fifteen minutes later they pulled out of Flamingo heading toward Miami.

Just after they passed the Mahogany Hammock turnoff, Mike shouted, "Look there!" pointing to the right out the windshield.

They both saw it clearly in the dry area to the south. A tiger. It was a small female. She looked young and didn't seem to be afraid of the truck.

Randy slowed the truck and handed his cell phone to Mike. "Take a couple of pictures of that will you? I want the folks back at Flamingo to see this."

"Are you going to send the pictures back to them when you call this in?"

"I don't see any point in calling it in. No one there is in any position to come out here and do anything but get another look at it. If you get some good pictures I'll surprise everyone when I get back this evening with a little slide show."

The animal started to move toward them. There was no menace. She looked like she was just coming over to say hello. Mike snapped about 10 shots as the animal sauntered their way.

"What the hell is this about?" exclaimed Mike, surprised by the animal's approach.

"I don't know, but I hear there was a sighting in this area where the tiger acted like it wanted to be friends. Maybe this is the animal they were talking about. Maybe it was a pet. Anyway I'm not stopping. We have to get you to Miami. I'll let everyone know all about this when I get back to Flamingo tonight."

"I finally am getting hungry," Mike said. "I hope there's some good food at the airport."

"If you don't find anything there, you can always ask for a second cracker once you're airborne," quipped Randy as they drove on, leaving the tiger standing in the road looking after the disappearing truck.

26

Shelly found Jake in the conference room with Steve mulling over some of the conversations they'd had with other field biologists who might be able to help with the population studies.

"Hi guys," she started off. "Jake, I have a couple of requests. I know I got off on the wrong foot with you dissing your outfit but I hope you'll accept my apology on that. I am sorry. I do run into field people at the museum but when I see them they are back in the city and in button-down plaid shirts and sneakers."

"OK," said Jake, not sounding any too accepting of the apology.

"Anyway, the superintendent showed me where we could work and it is very bare bones. We will have a sink but that's about it for a wet lab. I called the University of Miami and made arrangements to use one of their portable PCR kits and microsatellite analyzers. There would be some added chemicals and other equipment too from them for collecting samples. We'll have to order the primers and replacement chemicals and get them overnighted, but we can get it going once it's all here."

"So what do you need from me?"

"Could we ask Randy to pick up all the equipment and chemicals from the University once he drops off Mike at the airport? It would save a second trip up there."

"Sure, I'll give him a call or you can since you work with him. No problem. What else?"

"This one's a little more delicate. I was wondering now that Mike is no longer with you if you could let Randy stay in your camper with you. He and I get along really well and I have no problem rooming with a guy. It's just that I am so used to living alone that having him there all the time even when we're not working is hard for me."

After a pause Jake nodded saying, "OK I guess. Can he cook?"

"Not that I know about but as far as I can tell he doesn't snore if that helps. Thanks so much. I'll call Randy and give him more specifics about the labs where he needs to pick things up for us and the names of my contacts there. I'll also give him a heads up about his move to your camper."

Shelly stepped out into the hall and called Randy on his cell. He had parked at the airport and was having a late lunch with Mike before his plane. He told her he had a surprise for everyone when he got back later. He would pick up some groceries at Publix and all of the lab supplies at U. of M. and head back. She also told him about his impending move to Jake's RV. Shelly seemed a little taken aback when Randy didn't sound at all surprised by that. Maybe she'd been more obviously annoyed with having to share space than she had thought.

Shelly stuck her head back into the conference room to let Jake and Steve know about her conversation with Randy, and then headed back to her camper to catch up on some notes, some planning and some reading.

Shelly heard the truck pulling in around dusk. She headed out toward Jake's camper dressed in long clothes and sprayed down for the swarms of insects she now understood would greet her. As she got closer to the truck she stopped cold, seriously considering turning around and running. But maybe just backing slowly to her own camper would be a better idea. Beside the truck Jake and Randy stood talking calmly. Up in the truck bed stood a large, seemingly docile tiger.

This was much more of a surprise than she thought Randy had been hinting about.

27

"I just got off the phone with Florida Fish and Wildlife," said Steve. It was just after dusk and he was back in the conference room with the superintendent, reviewing where things stood. "We talked through a lot of things but I did ask them about the panther status in South Florida. They say the population of panthers out here is between 100 and 160. They have real trouble getting more precise counts.

"They get about 30 reports every year of human panther interactions. I don't want to jump to conclusions, but if we add up all of the numbers for tiger sightings, we get between 20 and 30. If there is some parallel to the panther numbers, we could be looking at a sizable population out there. If, if, if."

"Some of those panther interactions are sightings or road kills on Route 29, Alligator Alley or the Tamiami Trail. We don't have any reports of those kinds of incidents with tigers. Wouldn't that suggest their population would be much smaller?" asked the superintendent.

"Not necessarily. Tigers are very wary. These animals have been around humans and maybe even vehicles and learned how to avoid them. This is a new environment for them so they may be extra cautious. Over the last decade or so, the state developed wildlife crossings to minimize those kinds of interactions along the roads. The crossings mostly go under the roads and seem to be working pretty well for a lot of animals. And we just opened the Florida wildlife corridor, that contiguous stretch of wild land from Flamingo to the Georgia border and over into the Panhandle. If tigers are using pieces of that here in the Glades, it's unlikely they would run into people or encounter a road."

"Doesn't that corridor suggest they might not just be in the Glades? They could be all over the state."

"I doubt it. We would have heard something from elsewhere if they were. But it does mean we have to shut down the crossings and block the corridor before they do start using other areas."

"That won't be easy. It's tantamount to securing the US/Mexico border. You know how well that's been going.

"I've been thinking about the citizen science involvement again and wondering if we could enlist some of the people out there in the Gold Coast area or the Naples/Everglades City region who own personal drones to do some aerial camera surveys. They might be able to do that from closed vehicles, making it safe enough to have them help."

"Drone surveys sound like a good idea. I'm surprised we didn't think about that during our meeting earlier. I'll look into that and get back to you."

"I'm also concerned that if we have trouble keeping these animals contained in the park we probably have an equal or worse problem keeping people out. The park perimeter is amazingly porous where people are concerned. Since we are getting so much play in the press around these animals it could have the effect of drawing in the curious and the crazies. One more incident could bring us some really negative fallout."

"What can we do about that?" Steve wondered.

"Nothing I can think of," said the superintendent, wandering over to the window.

"Good Christ look at that!" he exclaimed looking out toward the camping area.

Steve ran over to the window and stared out mouth agape. They were looking at the same scene Shelly was slowly backing away from.

28

Saul Birnberg had been the "Miami Sun Times" environmental staff writer for over a decade. He had come out of journalism school with a minor in geology and fit naturally into the slot of writing about Florida's continuing struggle between its environmental concerns and economic development.

He had been following the electronic media reports about finding tigers in the Everglades and had made several unsuccessful attempts to get interviews with National Park people and politicians who might have some say in decision making about what was to be done about them. So far he had been turned away. Now he was in the office of his editor-in-chief, who wanted to talk to him about just that issue.

"I just got off the phone with the park superintendent at Everglades. They're not allowing the media into the park until further notice. They said they would release information daily at press conferences up at Shark Valley where media people from most of Florida could get to most easily. They told me that they would allow one print journalist and one photographer to go out with the teams at Flamingo where they are headquartering the rest of the efforts, well out of the way of the public and media frenzy, for first-hand reporting in feature articles. They wanted assurances that whoever went out would follow their rules to the letter. We were among about six outlets that put in proposals for the job. Luckily they chose us. That hopefully will mean major feature reporting and it could mean awards in the end for all of us. Ready to dive in?"

"You bet. Who's the photographer?"

"That's your call. You know the work of every staff photog, so pick the one you think will give you the best pictures for this kind of story."

"When do we go?"

"As soon as you can get packed up. They're getting ready to start surveys and have people lined up from all over to help. How soon can you be ready?"

"I'd say about an hour for me once I get home to pack. I'll ask Kim Hudson to go with me for the photographs. She's great with outdoor assignments and she runs, bikes and kayaks all the time. This should be right up her alley.

"By the way, where do we go and where do we stay?"

"They're running everything through Flamingo in the park so go there. I'll have one of our staff rent you an RV. Since you're taking Kim I'll be sure it's one with separate sleeping areas for privacy and some good work surfaces for two people. I'll call your cell when I have details on the rental. I'll put the RV in your name but I'll put Kim on there as a driver, too. Remember this is only marginally an exclusive. Everything you learn there will probably be shared with every other media outlet around at those press conferences. You're just getting the first-hand look at the whole project. So find the good stories that'll differentiate us from them."

"We'll get them for sure. We may even bring back a tiger for an office pet."

"Don't you dare! Just get it done and get it done well. I know you two will do us proud. Enjoy."

29

While they had been standing out by the truck talking, the tiger remained staring down at them. Steve had called Jake's cell phone at that point, thinking that was a whole lot better than risking going over there to find out what was going on. Jake had told him that as far as he could tell, there was no danger from the tiger, and Steve should come on over and meet her.

When Steve got to the truck the tiger remained in the truck bed and merely looked him over from there. Steve's first word was, "Well...?"

"Go ahead and tell him the story, Randy."

Randy related how he and Mike had seen the tiger on the way to Miami. It hadn't seemed aggressive or afraid of the truck or them but they hadn't taken the time to stop in all the excitement, but they had taken pictures of the animal. He hadn't called it in since there was no way anyone could do anything about it, so he wanted to surprise everyone with the pictures when he got back. After Randy dropped Mike and picked up the equipment at U. of M., he headed to Publix and got a big load of food for the two RV's. On the way back the tiger showed up again, right around the same turnoff.

Since he was alone, Randy was really cautious, but he did pull off the road thinking he could get some better photos on his cellphone. The tiger just ambled over to the truck, rubbed against the hood like a house cat, and then came up to the cab, stood on its back legs and looked in the window. Randy said he could almost have sworn that the animal smiled at him.

The tiger seemed to take in everything in the truck and then gently scratched at the door. Randy had taken a chance and gotten one of the whole roasting chickens he had bought at

Publix out of the cooler on the front seat, cracked the window and tossed it out toward the tiger.

The animal had wolfed down the chicken in a flash and was back at the window seemingly looking for more. Randy then threw her another one which she ate with abandon. At that point the tiger lay down beside the truck and started to groom herself.

Randy knew it was possibly the most stupid thing he'd ever done but he opened the door slowly and eased out of the truck. When the tiger stood up he almost panicked and jumped back in the cab and shut the door. There was something in this animal's demeanor that stopped him, however.

The tiger eased closer and rubbed her head on his leg and then licked his pants with her incredibly rough tongue. While tigers don't purr like house cats, he could imagine the animal doing just that, after seeing all of these behaviors that reminded him of pet cats he'd had growing up.

Randy had then taken a chance and opened the tailgate to the truck. Almost immediately, the tiger leapt up into the bed and stood staring out over the cab as if it were ready to move on with the truck. Randy had gotten back in the cab and come straight back to Flamingo.

"So this girl was undoubtedly a pet. It looks like she may have been hand raised from a cub, too. I know those performers with the tigers out in Las Vegas have them trained to be docile and uncaged most of the time, but one did attack its owner a few years ago. Let's hope that doesn't happen here," said Jake.

"As friendly as she seems, we will have to keep her caged or restricted just because she probably will be just as unpredictable as any other wild animal that's been trained to be a pet," said Steve.

"In any case I've named her Tonya and she can be our project mascot, caged or not," Randy replied.

"This does beg the question, though," Steve continued, "if we are going to live-trap these animals and try to relocate them someplace, just where are we going to take them? And we still have no idea how many of these animals we're talking about. So far, live-trapping hasn't been very successful."

"We called the Big Cat Rescue up in Tampa and they may be able to take some cats themselves, but they are very limited in terms of space and resources," Randy said.

"I'll contact the American Zoo and Aquarium Association and see if they can help us on that score." added Jake. "I also have a contact in the zoo program up at Santa Fe Community College in Gainesville who might have some suggestions or know who to talk to. In the meantime, we probably ought to get some kind of sample for DNA analysis and get Shelly on that. Do you suppose she'll come out of the RV when she sees Tonya out here, Randy?"

"I'd bet not," Randy replied opening the tailgate and letting Tonya jump down into the campground.

"Do you still have the pictures on your cell phone?" asked Steve.

"Yeah I do. I did send a couple along with a "selfie" of Tonya and me and with a 'Hey look what I followed me home. Can I keep her?' message to my parents in Maine, though. Hope that was OK."

"I hope your folks won't think about sending them around to the press?" Steve asked.

"I have no idea but I hope not. I was just trying to be funny."

30

"So this morning the 'Bangor Star' posted a picture of a loose tiger at Flamingo in the Glades. Some museum intern working on the tiger issue sent it to his parents, and the wires and social media picked it up by noon," reported the governor's newly appointed aide. "I think you're going to have to address this thing sooner rather than later."

"What am I supposed to say and to whom, do you think?" he replied with a heavy dose of sarcasm.

"You need to explain how you hope the state will be allowed to help the feds with this problem and really play up the business of not letting that most important ecosystem get further compromised by this turn of events. You don't need to be very specific about what you plan to do, particularly if we set it up so you don't have to take questions from reporters. Could be a good photo op, too."

"Where are we going to do this?'"

"Undoubtedly the best place will be down in the Glades. We'll arrange it to be part of the park service's daily press briefing, with the stipulation that no questions be allowed. That is held at the National Park's Shark Valley Visitor's Center. That puts you in real proximity to a whole bunch of your big gift supporters in Naples. We'll combine your trip to the Glades with a fundraising excursion to the Naples area. It'll make the whole trip a real win."

"Go ahead and arrange it for tomorrow. And try not to bring me any more news about this. It's really wasting my time."

"I'm on it, sir," she said, backing out the door.

"Seems like I heard that line before somewhere," mumbled the governor.

31

"I'm Saul Birnberg and this is Kim Hudson. We're here from the 'Miami Sun Times.' We're your media reps on the tiger project."

Saul had his hand out to Shelly who had heard their RV coming into the campground and had come out to see who had been let into the park. Apparently Jake had heard them too because he had just stepped out of his RV and was headed their way. Randy had headed off earlier with Tonya to do something; Shelly had no idea what.

"I'm Shelly Lawson and the guy coming toward us who looks like an escapee from a Jack Hanna look-alike contest is Jake Ballard. If you saw a guy walking a tiger around the area on your way in his name is Randy and his tiger is named Tonya," Shelly said, extending her hand rather unenthusiastically.

Shelly had not been told there would be press people on this part of the project and really had no desire to have her work filter through some tabloid or another. She had seen too many articles in the popular media about the museum's work that were riddled with errors or half-truths and poorly explained information. It seemed to her that publicity was as often as not a fairly negative thing. She knew her supervisor wanted to highlight the museum nationally and bring it some needed exposure. She was certain she didn't want to be at the center of it, but she had no choice.

"Kim's a great photographer and loves all things outdoors. I'm the environmental staff writer just so you know why they sent us. We'll try to stay out of your hair but we will need to ask you questions as we go along to make sure our information is accurate. We really don't want be in the way, we just want to get good stories and pictures."

"Neither of us is really heading the work here, said Shelly. "So you'll want to talk to a ranger named Steve Hamilton up at the visitor center. Jake here is a field biologist volunteer from Florida Gulf Coast University and I'm on assignment from the

American Museum of Natural History in New York. When you see him, the tiger guy is with me."

"How about if Kim and I get set up, go meet with Steve Hamilton and talk to you two later? I should ask, is this tiger your friend has out and about something we should worry about?"

"She hasn't killed anyone yet. There's always going to be a first though."

Kim smiled, catching the sarcasm, but Shelly could see fear rise in Saul's eyes as he started to move away from the conversation group and toward their RV.

Once Saul and Kim had retreated, Shelly asked Jake, "Were you aware that they were allowing press in here to cover our work?"

"Yeah, Steve mentioned it to me earlier today."

"I would have appreciated it if someone would have let me know. Not that I could have done anything to change it, but it does give a person time to prepare for her close-up."

"I can see why you're miffed but I'm sure it was just a slip on Steve's part."

"And maybe yours since you could have told me, too."

"OK, mine too. Sorry."

Shelly didn't think Jake sounded sorry at all, just annoyed.

"It's hot out here and I'm going back in. You can stay out and get the sweat marks on your shirt a little more intense if you want. Talk to you later," Shelly said, turning back toward her RV.

"I think these sweat marks are a real fashion statement, lady!" thought Jake, tipping his hat with false charm.

32

"Steve, why are you letting this guy Randy walk around with a loose tiger? Couldn't it attack someone here?"

"We really have no choice, Saul. You heard the story of how Randy found Tonya and brought her here. We don't have cages or closed vehicles appropriate to getting her anywhere else at the moment. We don't have anywhere else to put her. Until we get some help on that, it seems best to let her hang out with Randy, who she's clearly bonded to. I can't see driving her into Miami or up the turnpike in the back of an open pickup, can you?"

"No, I guess not, but I'm not comfortable with her just being loose like that."

"That's going to have to be your problem for a while at least. We have more pressing issues to solve."

"When will we be briefed on what's going on?" Kim asked.

"We're doing our overview at tonight's press conference up in Shark Valley. You'll learn everything we know then as long as the governor doesn't take all night grandstanding beforehand. He wanted to be on the schedule for that briefing even though he knows precious little about what we're up against and probably cares even less. You didn't hear any of that from me - and write any of that down and I'll have you out of here in a flash!"

"OK, OK. How are we supposed to get up to that press conference? It's long trip."

"We've got it on interactive video and audio feed to here, Saul. You'll see it all from the conference room up at the visitor center starting at 4:30. We'll put you by an exit door way across the room from Randy and Tonya so you don't panic."

By 4:30, everyone except Randy and Tonya had been in the conference room for a long time. The conversation had been non-stop and you could almost smell the sense of urgency. Randy and Tonya came in at the last minute and stood together near the door farthest from the screen. Tonya sat down like a friendly dog and leaned into Randy, who had to brace himself against the wall to keep from falling over.

On screen everyone could see the park superintendent step up to the lectern and address the crowd of media people. TV camera lights came on and flashes went off everywhere.

"Thanks for coming, everyone. I'd also like to welcome the people down at Flamingo who are joining us on the audio/video feed you see to my left. As you know by now, over the last several weeks we have become aware that Everglades National Park has yet another exotic species problem. Tigers have been reported at several locations in the park and we have had two tiger-related deaths and possibly three. Because of that we have closed the park to the public indefinitely. Tonight we are going to tell you what we know and what our plans are for now.

"Before I get started, however, the governor has asked to say a few words about our problem here. He respectfully requests that you save your questions for us since we have been on the front lines of this issue from the beginning. Governor."

With that the governor strode on to the podium, grabbed the sides of the lectern and smiled broadly at the audience.

"Thanks so much for having me. As I'm sure everyone here is aware, we in state government view the Everglades as perhaps Florida's most important natural asset. We stand ready to help in any way we can to ensure that this essential and beautiful place is not compromised by these new invaders.

"I will be receiving briefings on the progress here at least twice a day until the problem is resolved. We will work with the

National Park Service and any of the other agencies involved in this effort to bring our state's resources to their aid. I came here in person today to show just how committed we are to helping.

"I've been assured that you will be informed with daily updates as the work on this problem continues. The people here are the experts and the ones to ask for details of every step in the process of eliminating this threat to our beautiful Everglades. As the superintendent mentioned, we in Tallahassee ask that you direct all your requests for information to them. They will fill you in on every aspect of our efforts at the state level to help, as well as the efforts of the many others involved.

"Thank you for having me tonight."

With that the governor left the podium smiling and waving to shouts of "Governor!" and "Just one question!" He remained silent as he left the building with his security. Only his new aide heard him mumble, "Hope that holds the bastards for a while."

33

National park borders are not easy to close off. The most accessible parts of the Everglades have roads and visitor centers or at least gates so that those entrances to the park can be controlled. Areas such as the Ten Thousand Islands, however, are accessible by boat from the Gulf of Mexico so are essentially open.

Ed, Jim and Hilary knew that they could leave from the marina north of Everglades City and wend their way to the Ten Thousand Islands without being spotted by park personnel or even the Coast Guard, which had been put on watch for that kind of activity once the park had been closed to the public.

Ed had just bought a used Blackfin up in Port Charlotte. While Ed wasn't really a fisherman, he did like this sport boat, and it had been rated as one of the best in its class ever made.

He had wanted to take it out somewhere for a couple of nights once he had made sure it was seaworthy and all the parts were working to his satisfaction. The boat was designed to sleep up to four. None of Ed's friends were fishermen either, but most of them did like boat trips. As it happened, Jim and Hilary had time off the same days as Ed.

They had talked of little else but the tiger sightings in the Everglades since the reports had hit the media. All three wanted to find one of the tigers and get some good pictures and bring back some good stories for future parties. They were bummed by the park closing. Last night over dinner and a lot of wine, they arrived at a plan to use Ed's boat to skirt the lookouts and head into the islands near where the first suspected tiger attack had occurred.

The boat could sleep all three but it would be hot out there. In the cabin, this boat had AC, a small fridge in the galley, and even a toilet and shower. It didn't take much to stock the boat for the trip. They decided to just wing it and not plan where to go.

They headed out into the Gulf just after an early supper as the day was cooling off just a little and the sea breezes were beginning to increase. Jim and Hilary immediately hit the wine cache while Ed stayed with his diet soda in case the Coast Guard saw them.

They slowly made their way offshore and then south for about an hour or so before turning east toward the islands. They thought they might get somewhere close to the area where that first tiger incident occurred and then spend the night before slowly cruising in and around the keys the next day, hoping to spot a tiger.

The seas were almost glass calm and the ride was smooth. Ed and Jim were barefoot and shirtless, catching as much of the breeze as possible and not having to worry at all about insects. Soon they were well out of sight of any other boaters and headed into the islands.

Because of the boat's depth sounder and sonar they were able to maneuver among the small keys in spite of the ever shifting sand bars. It was slow going but the engine was very quiet at these speeds. They hoped it would be quiet enough to not scare away any wildlife in the area, including a tiger.

Jim and Hilary were pretty buzzed by this time, and Ed was getting ready to drop the soda and join them since they hadn't seen another soul for a long time. As Ed eased the boat around a small key, Hilary stood up and pointed off to the north east. There on the shore where sand replaced the mangroves on the point of the key stood a large orange striped cat. This tiger was a male and about 500 pounds, though they didn't know that then. If they had looked carefully they would have seen that the cat's ribs were showing dramatically along its sides. This was a desperate, starving and very hungry animal.

The tiger looked straight at the boat and seemed to grimace at them, narrowing its eyes and baring its teeth. They heard no roar. It made no move toward or away from them either.

Ed eased the boat as slowly and quietly as he could toward the animal. Unfortunately he was paying way too much attention to the animal and none to the depth gauge. The crunch of the bow into a sandbar sent all three friends lurching forward. Ed was stopped by the wheel in the cockpit. Jim was thrown up against the gunnel and had the wind knocked out of him. Hilary was jolted forward into the cockpit.

The tiger eased its way into the water and moved their way. Ed reversed the engine but his initial try wasn't enough to dislodge the boat from the sand. The tiger was there. It stood up on its hind legs on the sandbar and grabbed Jim off the gunnel with its front claws digging deep into Jim's shoulders. Jim was screaming in pain and fear, having regained some wind. Ed and Hilary rushed out to grab Jim but missed him as the tiger splashed off with Jim thrashing and flailing now hanging from its mouth. It disappeared into the mangroves. The sound of Jim's screams faded with the increasing distance and then suddenly stopped.

Ed rushed back into the cockpit and tried to reverse the boat again before the animal came back after more. This time he got it right and the boat slid into deeper water. Hilary was hysterical with fear knowing that she had just witnessed one of her best friends being killed. Ed got the boat out into deeper water, put the engine in a neutral idle and then grabbed Hilary, holding her close, as much to calm himself as to calm her.

When they had stopped shaking and crying enough to act, Ed took a GPS reading and used the VHF to call the Coast Guard. Being cited for trespassing in a closed National Park was of no concern to him now.

34

"I'm going to turn over this session to Steve Hamilton who will be the lead on the tiger project from here on," continued the superintendent once the Governor had vacated the building. "Steve is working at our command post in Flamingo. Steve."

Steve positioned himself so he was center in the video feed to Shark Valley and began the briefing.

Steve began with a quick review of the information that had been released to the press up until this meeting. He wanted to be certain that everyone was on the same page with that information, whether they had all done their homework or not.

He continued, "What I can tell you at this point is that we are just about in a position with plans and personnel to start assessing the scope of the problem with tigers in the Everglades."

At that point a hand shot up and a question was shouted from the middle of the gathering in Shark Valley. "Why do you need to know the 'scope of the problem' before you actually start doing something about it?"

"The number of tigers out there will determine the scale of what we do to get them out of the park. It can also help us by determining if we need to keep the whole park closed or if we can safely open parts of it to the public."

"How are you going to go about this assessment?" came another question from the crowd.

"I'll cover some of that and probably some of the other questions you came in with this evening as I go along. If you'll give me a few minutes to go over what I have here then we can go to questions right after that."

None of the journalists in the Shark Valley center seemed satisfied with that approach but they didn't follow up with more shouted questions, either.

"Our number one goal is to keep people safe throughout this process," Steve continued. "Because of that we are using only people professionally trained in field work of this type. Many of our park people are good to go on this work and we have gotten some other scientists and technicians from organizations all around South and Central Florida. National and Florida Fish and Wildlife have brought us over a half dozen people and Audubon Florida and the Nature Conservancy also will have people in the field. We have Jake Ballard, a field biologist, from Florida Gulf Coast University who was the first to volunteer for this work, largely because he was with a friend and colleague when he first learned that it was a tiger attack in the Ten Thousand Islands. We've got requests into other universities for volunteer scientists to come and help, but frankly this is field season for academic people, and most of those researchers are out on their own projects and just not available.

"All of these folks will be conducting surveys 'on the ground' which really means mostly in the water in this park. They'll be looking for any signs that tigers are present in an area and they will be collecting samples of physical and biological material that can be analyzed for evidence of tigers. That includes things like fur samples, paw prints, dung, and remains of animals killed by a predator that might contain DNA from that predator. Those pieces of evidence will be analyzed here at Flamingo by Shelly Lawson and Randy Benoit from the American Museum of Natural History who are down here because they were the ones who linked our first samples to tigers."

Steve had moved the little camera that he had been standing in front of to show Shelly sitting in the conference room. He was careful not to let the image sent to the reporters in Shark Valley include Randy and Tonya. He knew the furor that showing Tonya would create, and he needed this session to go as smoothly as possible.

"We've been in contact with...."

At that point, a ranger rushed into the Shark Valley gathering and shouted. "There's been another kill in the Ten Thousand Islands close to the first one."

The crowd rose to their feet and surrounded the ranger, shouting questions and taking pictures, totally oblivious to Steve or anyone else who was supposed to be talking to them. The press conference was over.

35

"Why is Tonya still here and just wandering around loose?" asked Saul. "Why isn't she in a zoo or a sanctuary or something or at least in a pen here if she has to be here?"

"It's a lot easier for her to find food just wandering around, like the odd reporter for instance," quipped Shelly.

Everyone laughed except Saul. Steve explained. "We've tried a number of the usual channels to find a place for her but every place is full. Most have even started to divest themselves of some of their big cats because they are so expensive to keep and their budgets are being eviscerated. We haven't been able to get a pen big enough to make an animal this big comfortable down here. I think we've been through this before, Saul."

"Well where does she sleep?"

"She beds down outside Jake's RV where Randy sleeps and waits for him to come out and play. If you're worried, just don't go wandering around at night when Randy is inside. Like Shelly said, if we don't see you for a couple of hours we'll have Kim call your next of kin."

"Well what does she eat, then?"

"You really are a nervous Nelly. Are you sure you're an environmental reporter?" But before Saul could respond Steve added, "Actually we sourced food from the suppliers they use at the Miami Zoo. A truck is due to come in later this afternoon with food for Tonya and a whole bunch for us too along with some other equipment we put in for. I think you need to relax."

"As long as we're not getting anywhere with that press conference, why don't we get started doing something." Jake was getting even more impatient with what he saw as the glacial pace of this whole effort. "How about we take one of the pontoon boats up the canal to Coot Bay and maybe beyond if we have time. We can look for signs and take some samples so Shelly can get started as soon as the primers and chemicals arrive with the food."

"Yeah, OK," said Steve. "Randy, you and Tonya better stay here. We don't know how she will do on a boat or if we run into any other tigers. You can also take care of all the stuff coming in this afternoon. I'll get one of the boats ready and see anyone who wants to go at the docks in about a half hour."

"Saul and I will be there," said Kim.

"Not having the materials I need for lab work gives me the perfect excuse to be outside in the heat and the bugs for a few hours enjoying a cruise in the swamp, so I guess I'll go too," Shelly said somewhat reluctantly.

"Bring that cannon of yours, Jake," added Steve. "Make sure it's loaded."

36

Karl had no idea why he was being called back from the hunt to talk to the head wildlife manager. As the lead guide at the King Ranch Hunting Lodge, he was used to being on his own most of the time with the guests. He got most of the information on clients through emails and text messages from the front office. He was expected to make their hunting trip a perfect adventure. The clients were delivered to him soon after they had arrived by private jet. He almost never spoke to anyone in administration. They trusted him to treat every guest like royalty and make certain that they left with all the big game trophies they came expecting to get. Karl hadn't disappointed anyone in his nine years on the job. Most often he had made certain that the guests' experience was better than their expectations.

"We got a call from the Florida governor you had out last fall with his cronies. He remembered how good you were out there.

He said he has the big nilgai and cull buck heads on the wall of his den in the mansion, and he gets great comments on them all the time."

The manager hadn't even engaged in the usual "Howz it goin' out there?" you would expect just stepping into his office for the first time in months. Must be something special going down, thought Karl.

"So what's he want? Can't be just another boondoggle trip if you're calling me into talk about it."

"You're right. It isn't. You probably heard about the possible tiger problem they have in the Everglades, right?"

"I've read about it, yeah."

"Well the governor's handlers have suggested he do something proactive rather than waiting for the feds and others to go through channels. He wants to look like a hero to his electorate in the face of slow-paced bureaucratic responses."

"So how do we fit in?"

"Not we, Karl. You. The governor is really coming hard at the feds, his state people and even the non-profits to get them to allow him to protect Florida citizens from the 'man-eater of the Ten Thousand Islands' as he calls it."

"Why us here in Texas? He's got great resources in his own state."

"He really liked you and he can get his buddies at Big Sugar to run interference on almost all fronts for him. He can also expect some great funding from them for this effort of his. They know us and use us all the time for political junkets."

"Just what is this effort of his?"

"He wants you to come over there and kill the tiger in the Ten Thousand Islands that has taken out two people and generated a lot of bad press and fear. He wants you to do it very visibly so he gets maximum press on how he brought in the best big game hunter in the states to protect the citizens of Florida. He wants this to become the model for how his state will respond to any threat from nature."

"What about all the licensing and permissions for this kind of thing? If I'm going to do this it's got to be or at least look as legit as possible, or there will be a lot hitting the fan when I bring the animal back."

"It'll all be taken care of. He is the governor and he has clout all the way through the state and into D.C. too. We probably will take some heat from the conservation people but that'll be his problem to sort out. We get enough of that on our own here, anyway."

"So when do I do this?"

"ASAP. Pack up and we'll have the Gulfstream ready to get you there whenever you're ready. You'll be staying in Naples with one of the Sugar Daddies. He's got a mansion on the water and some great entertainment lined up for you."

"Just what kind of entertainment?"

"The kind where you shouldn't take pictures while it's happening. Now get outta here."

37

Randy and Tonya watched the refrigerated panel truck slowly make its way toward the visitor center. It slowed even further once the driver saw Tonya standing beside Randy. When the truck stopped it was still 20 feet from them. The driver just barely cracked the window in order to speak.

"Is it safe for you to be out there like that with that animal?"

"Seems to be. We've not seen anything from her to hint that we shouldn't feel safe. Are you OK delivering the stuff?"

"I'm not sure. Where does it go? Do I have to get close to that thing?"

"I could show you where to put things and I'll take Tonya, that's her name, elsewhere while you unload the truck. If you can get comfortable enough, I can stick around and help you unload. Your choice."

"Give me a minute."

Randy wasn't sure what the guy was going to do with his minute, but he waited patiently anyway.

"Well, OK. You can help. How do I make friends with, uhhh, Tonya?"

"Try doing what you would do with a strange dog. Just let her sniff your hand before you try to get out of the truck. Then move smoothly. Try not to seem afraid even if you are and don't make sudden movements. We think she's still got a bit of kitten in her and might like to play if she thinks you want to."

"Where are we taking all this stuff?"

"I'll walk over to where we'll unload it and then we can move it to specific places in that building once we get most of it off the truck. If you have some tiger food thawed out in there, it might make her even happier while we work."

With that, Randy and Tonya walked over to the entrance closest to the fridge and freezer units they were using for food, primers and chemicals, and they propped open the door.

The driver pulled out a haunch of meat that was cold but not frozen and flung it to the ground through the open window of the truck before he stepped down. Tonya was immediately deliriously happy and paid Randy and the driver little mind for the next half hour while they unloaded the truck. They got everything placed where it belonged, and the driver got in his truck as fast as possible and got ready to leave.

"That should hold you for a couple of weeks since there aren't many of you out here. Just give a holler when you need another order. I'll let the other drivers know about the cat if I'm not the one bringing it out here. Good luck with the project."

With that he put the truck in gear and headed back toward Miami.

Randy picked up his laptop and walked over to where Tonya had lain down after her meal. She seemed really satisfied and comfortable. Randy sat on the ground with his back up against a tree. Tonya stood up and walked over to some bare ground and started to roll in the dirt. He could have sworn he saw her smile.

He had an email waiting from the park superintendent. Somehow they had heard that he was good at looking for patterns in visual data. Maybe it was just because he had been the first to see the paw print in the drawings Shelly's computer had generated from the evidence gathered at the scene of the first incident. The super was asking him to take the lead, at Flamingo at least, on analyzing visual data from drones, aerial surveys from helicopters, and satellite imagery. Others would be doing the same with the same data at other sites throughout the park. That was quite a surprise. He was just an intern after all, but somehow he was seen as a real member of this team. He could do most of it outside with Tonya or with her in the Center with him after everyone had left for the night. He shot back a message of acceptance in a matter of minutes.

"Well Tonya, we're players now, babes," he said, patting her head.

38

Steve had a small electric motor on the boat they were using to keep things quiet. He wasn't sure whether motor noise would scare away any tigers or attract them but he did think that quiet was the best choice to start with. It had been over a year since he had been on one of these boats and even longer since he had been up the Flamingo Canal. Mainly Steve had done surveys of mammals and birds and hunted pythons with radio tags from roads. He was as glad to be getting out in the field as Jake seemed to be. Luckily, this late in the day the heat was moderating at least a little.

As everyone began to gather, Kim started shooting pictures of everything. It was hard to see any picture-worthy settings or activities, but she burned a lot of megabytes anyway. Saul showed up with a paper notebook and pencils tucked into a small shoulder bag with water bottles and power bars. Clearly he didn't trust electronic recording in this environment, or maybe he had just never discovered the joys of portable electronics in the field.

Shelly had outfitted herself in the lightest long clothes she could find and smelled strongly of citrusy insect repellent. She sported a wide-brimmed hat with mosquito netting tucked up over the brim.

"I'm ready for my trip down river, Mr. Allnutt," she said in her best Katherine Hepburn voice while climbing aboard.

"Here we are going down that river like Anthony and Cleopatra, Miss," came a reply from Jake who had just come up behind her and did his best to match her Hepburn with his Bogart.

"Remember, 'Nature, Mr. Allnutt, is what we are put in this world to rise above,'" Shelly/Hepburn rejoined.

By now everyone was smiling, and there seemed to be a new sense of camaraderie brewing just based on this simple exchange.

Once everyone had a seat, Steve started the motor and glided the boat slowly and almost silently away from the Marina and into the canal.

"What are we looking for, specifically?" asked Saul.

"Jake and I will be mostly looking for anything that is out of the ordinary and for obvious evidence of large-animal activity. We'll also be listening for sounds that could be made by our tigers. We can try to record anything like that on our phones. I brought a camera too. You, Shelly?"

"I have sampling supplies so I can get water and sediment samples if there are any places you guys think might have had tiger activity. I'll PCR it when I'm back in the lab to see if I can detect tiger DNA."

"You really think you can detect tiger DNA in water and sediment?" Saul asked.

"I think so. We won't know for sure until we try, but this can be pretty sensitive. In fact, that's why I'm using sterile supplies and gloves to collect samples. Since we've all been around Tonya, we probably have her hair and dander on us somewhere. If any of that got into a sample we would get a positive for tiger even if there wasn't one contributing to the sample. Even one cell from dander could screw up the sample."

Jake took in that explanation and realized why his sampling had not been very useful for PCR before. He remembered back to the sampling done after the sighting at Shark Valley and the sterile packaging for the collection bottle and the gloves the woman who collected the hair had used to retrieve that sample.

"Keep in mind this is our first crack at this survey, so we are trying things that we hope will help, but they may not pan out," Steve explained.

The boat slid under the Main Park Road leaving practically no wake. There were far fewer birds to be seen as they moved along than anyone would have thought. Steve knew this was most likely due to the pythons which had run low on food once they had decimated the small mammal populations in the park. They had moved on to the birds and were systematically eliminating them, too.

"Remind me again why you need to have any idea of how many animals are out here before you start doing something about them," asked Saul.

"Knowing the scope of any problem allows you to gauge the nature and scale of any response to it. It can give us a sense of whether we may be able to eliminate it or just control it. It can even tell us it is too far out of control for either course."

"You think this could be that far out of control?" asked Kim.

"It certainly is with a number of our invasives in the park already, Kim. Pythons, a bunch of different plant species, and some things we haven't even begun to survey really are totally out of control. We keep trying to manage them but we aren't winning those battles."

"Is it mostly a matter of money, Steve?"

"Money figures in strongly, Shelly, but that's not the whole problem. Sometimes you can throw a crap-load of resources at a problem and still get nowhere. And you have to be careful about what you use to control things, even if you decide you have a shot at doing that."

"Won't these things just use up all the resources and then die out? Couldn't you just leave it all alone and let it get back to normal on its own?"

"Doesn't work that way, Saul," said Jake. "These organisms get to an equilibrium with their new environment. That becomes the new 'normal' that is light years away from what was here before."

"There are plenty of dangers in other parks and people die all the time in them. So why close this park now, Steve?"

"Those dangers are known quantities, Saul. We know how to warn people about those. We have a sense of where they are, when they might occur, and how to minimize their risk. What we can't do is stop people from being stupid. We can move an aggressive bear but we can't stop a dumb tourist from harassing one. Most importantly, here we don't have any idea of the scope of the problem or what to do to protect people from tigers or themselves yet."

After a couple of minutes Steve said, "Hey guys, I'm seeing some things here we need to be paying attention to. Jake, are you seeing what I'm seeing as we're moving along?"

"If you mean the pushed down grass like large animal paths along the banks here, yeah. I don't see that kind of thing in other sawgrass I've been through."

"That's what I mean. Shelly, how about taking some samples from several of the areas near those paths as we pass. I'll give you GPS readings for each stop if you can write them down on the sample bottles. Kim, can you get pictures each time so we can look at these again back at the center?"

"Sure thing, Steve."

Steve guided the boat to the closest of the possible paths. Shelly donned gloves and got sample bottles ready. Kim angled for the best pictures of the grass and the activity on the boat. Saul took notes like a madman.

"I don't think we need to even do a PCR on this little sample," said Shelly. She held up a sample jar in which she had collected a large clump of orange fur from the teeth of one of the grass blades. "I think we found a tiger trail."

39

"I'm looking for Ed Tillinghast," Karl said to the only person he had run into at the marina in Naples where he had been directed. He was looking for the guy who owned the boat that had been attacked recently by the tiger.

"Might have seen him. Who the hell are you to ask anyway?" came the reply from the man who was taking the cover off the cockpit of his sailboat.

"I'm here on the governor's orders about that tiger in the Glades he ran into, if you must know."

"Just checkin', buddy. I like being a bit careful with people who just show up randomly around here. Don't want any more reporters down here either. I saw Ed about 20 minutes ago down by his boat. It's the Blackfin in the last slip along here. No name on it though. I didn't see him leave so he might still be down there."

"Thanks."

Karl made his way down the docks to the last slip where the Blackfin was moored. He didn't see anyone at first or hear any sounds. He had heard that people got really ticked off if you just boarded their boat without being asked so he just shouted.

"Hey Ed! You in there?"

A head popped out from below with an "I'm here." Followed quickly by, "And who the hell are you? Not another reporter I hope. If you are just get out of here now!"

"No, Ed. I'm no reporter. I'm here on orders from the governor. Here's a letter of introduction explaining."

Karl handed Ed a note on official stationary from the governor's office.

"Karl Messer huh? So what do you want with me? It doesn't say here what you do or why you're here."

"I'm a big game hunting guide with the King Ranch in Texas. The governor brought me out here to kill that tiger that attacked your boat. He wants the kill widely publicized. You know, so he can show he's doing all he can to keep the public safe. They told me you not only could get me to the place where the tiger came after your boat but you'd do it without getting stopped by the Coast Guard or any other enforcement people."

"So what you're telling me is that you really don't have any official approval to do this. You are just some hired gun from Texas here to make the governor look good."

"You could put it that way. Really the governor is getting all the approvals for this but they aren't in place just yet. Once we have the cat strapped on to your boat like a hood ornament, though, it should be no problem for people to see that this was the right thing to do for public safety. I'm sure he'll get all the paper work sorted out though."

"Who told you I could get you past the authorities?"

"The people I'm staying with in town here. You don't need to know who they are."

"I would love to see that cat dead. He killed my best friend out there. The problem is that the Coast Guard and the police have been all over me since I came back to the marina. I haven't seen anyone today except you but if I take the boat out they will probably send out an all-points wondering what the hell I'm up to."

"So you don't think you can get me out there then?"

"I didn't say that. Just talking out loud. We can do it. But we have to leave in the middle of the night and very slowly so we can be really quiet."

"How about tonight?"

"You got it. I'll plan to sleep aboard tonight so no one will expect me around town. Be here about 3:00 am. Just come aboard. Don't call or anything. I'll be here and ready."

"I'll have some serious equipment with me, if you know what I mean."

"I should hope so! Can't wait."

40

"And me without my guitar and tie-dyed T-shirt. Go figure," said Shelly settling down in a camp chair near the fire ring where the rest of the crew, including Randy and Tonya, had gathered after dinner for an evening out of the RVs. The fire served the purposes of keeping the insects at bay and giving just enough flickering light so that everyone could see everyone else in the serious dark of the campground. It certainly wasn't needed for warmth. The heat and humidity of the day lingered as usual this time of year, even after the typical late afternoon tropical thunderstorms that had rumbled through earlier. Most everyone smiled at Shelly's sarcasm.

Saul had positioned himself as far away from Randy and Tonya as he could without looking too foolish. Kim had compensated for her co-worker by sitting next to Tonya. She had her camera with her even though it was very dark, clearly ready for anything.

"When we got back I alerted the other team leaders what we had seen out there this evening," Steve reported. "Now at least we all have some visual clues to look for every time we go out."

"This is great for the aerial survey pictures I'm working with, too," chimed in Randy. "I can be looking for large trails in the grasses that wouldn't normally be there and see where they lead."

"I'll have the PCR on that sample we got today done by tomorrow afternoon. Hopefully that will give us some more information to go on," added Shelly. "I'm actually looking forward to getting more samples from other teams around the park. It feels like we're actually doing something, finally."

"I know what you mean," Jake added. "I've been chomping at the bit to do just about anything since we got here. I wish we had more field equipment for remote monitoring like camera traps and sound-activated recorders, but I guess there just aren't that many of those to go around, right Steve?"

"We sent out requests all over the place to borrow more, but so far what we already own is all we've got to work with."

After a bit of a lull with everyone staring into the fire seemingly somewhat mesmerized, Shelly asked, "What got you into photojournalism, Kim?"

Kim was a bit taken by surprise that anyone would ask her that. She was used to the negative responses of almost everyone she encountered except the ego-driven media hogs. Somehow the concept of paparazzi had poisoned perceptions of her line of work. She certainly didn't mind people asking, though.

"When I got to college I knew I wanted to do something in the arts but I didn't know what, at first. By the time I was a junior, though, I had tried lots of media and styles that I thought I liked and some I thought I hated. Nothing felt right to me. That spring I took a class in fine art photography and something clicked. Sorry, I really didn't mean to pun there."

"That's OK. Puns are better than some other people's sarcasm," Jake added, clearly directing the comment at Shelly but with a wry smile.

"I'll try to keep them to a minimum so my story has transparency," Kim added, unable to stop herself.

"After that I took a bunch of other photography courses and loved them all. The school had a great photojournalism department but I only tried a couple of courses there. I was really set on being an artist, not a journalist."

"What changed your mind?" Randy asked.

"After I left New Haven I started working in some studios that did fashion photography. I mainly free-lanced on a contract basis so it allowed me to do that work and also try some more artsy stuff on my own during the shoots. I even had some success at it."

"What do you mean by 'some success'?" asked Steve.

"I wound up being carried in a couple of galleries in New York and LA and I was making a good living on the art and free-lancing fashion shoots. Then I was asked to be part of an exhibit at BAM."

"Brooklyn Academy of Music?" Shelly asked.

"Yes, that BAM. The exhibit was a few years ago but it became the turning point for me."

"What was the exhibit? I may have seen it. I go there all the time." Shelly said.

"It was called "Modern Fashion in Black and White" and it featured about six of us who shot artsy fashion shots in black and white featuring models of all ethnicities. It got good press and even some awards."

"I did see that show. It was wonderful. I wish I could remember the specifics so I could recall which images were yours."

"Sometimes I don't even recall those images myself, Shelly. After the nonsense of the opening and all the hoopla surrounding the exhibit, it all just started to feel more empty than energizing. I had grown up in the country and outdoors most of the time, and now I was almost always in deep urban environments with people I didn't like all that much. I thought back to some of my classes and started to rethink where I wanted to take my skills.

"I have always loved storytelling but I'm not a good writer. After about a year of flopping around not really enjoying myself anymore I thought about giving photojournalism a try. I hadn't loved those classes but they did talk a lot in there about telling stories with pictures, the best ones telling a whole story with just one good picture. I went to the libraries and started looking at photos from the time of Matthew Brady to now. So I thought I'd give it a try.

"I didn't think war photography would be such a blast. Sorry. And geopolitical work seemed like a real snore to me. When I thought back to growing up and how much I liked being outdoors all the time I naturally sorry again latched on to environmental subjects. So that's the tale."

"Great story to hear, Kim. We've been working together for how many years now? And I didn't know any of that."

"No worries, Saul. A photojournalist is only as relevant as her most recent best picture. No reason anyone would care about how I got here. But tomorrow night it is your turn to tell your story. As for me, I'm done for the night and plan to turn in and read for a while."

"Sounds good," said Shelly, as everyone nodded agreement. "Tomorrow I'll bring the marshmallows if we can get other volunteers for the graham crackers and chocolate bars."

"You're on. We'll make it happen. And I have it on good authority that s'mores go great with wine. Any volunteers for sommelier of the evening?" Steve added.

"I think I have some spare altar wine from St. Ohmygods parish or somewhere back in the trailer. Should go great with those things," said Jake with a smile.

"Tonya and I've got the fire, guys," Randy added. "See you all tomorrow."

41

Karl Messer had boarded Ed's boat at 3:05 am and unpacked a Weatherby .378 Magnum bolt action rifle with a Nikon 3x9x40m scope. Ed was duly impressed. The Yukon night vision binoculars were icing on the cake.

They slipped out of the marina as slowly as Ed's boat would go, which meant practically no noise or wake at all. By the time they were out of sight of land and well south of the marina, Ed opened it up a bit and got them headed toward the 10,000 islands. He had kept as few lights on as possible and for all intents and purposes, he had navigated the whole distance as a dark shadow moving against a darker sea.

By the time the sun was up, they were stopped not far from where Ed and his pals had run into their tiger. He got the boat as close to the islands they passed among as possible, this time keeping a very close eye on the depth finder. By now the night vision binoculars were not necessary. Karl sat almost impassively at the stern surveying the islands and sandbars as they passed.

"There!" Karl said in a tense but quiet voice and pointed to the island just to the left of the bow. There on the sandy edge stood a tiger. A big one.

Ed thought he recognized it as the one who killed his friend, but he couldn't be sure. It had all happened so fast back then, and he had a lot of things on his mind other than what the damn tiger looked like.

Karl told Ed in hushed tones how to approach the animal. He chambered a round as quietly as possible and waited for Ed to cut the engine to minimize vibrations which could throw off his accuracy. The tiger didn't move. It stood there staring at the boat with little sign of any response to it.

Karl wanted to take the animal with one shot. If possible he wanted to hit it in the front left part of the chest where only an entry wound would mar the pelt. This would mean that the head would be good for mounting and the skin would make a great souvenir. Since the animal looked to be a male, he was sure he could sell the genitals to Chinese black-market people for good money, too. Karl chambered his round as quietly as he could, knowing the sound would carry too well over water.

Ed positioned the boat and cut the engine. The boat settled quietly on the calm water. The tiger didn't move and didn't respond. Karl crouched down and steadied the rifle on the gunnel. When he fired Ed jumped, not expecting quite the sound he heard.

The tiger seemed to startle and yet rather than showing that on its face, those muscles seemed to go slack. It fell where it had stood.

It took Karl and Ed some extraordinary effort to get the dead animal strapped on to the side of the boat. It was heavy. Both men were sweating profusely by the time Ed was able to crank up the engine and start heading back north.

The Coast Guard boat was right alongside the Blackfin as they entered the marina. They had picked up the boat about 10 miles out and immediately had Ed power it down. Karl had assured Ed that he had connections, and now that there was a dead man-eater on board, the Coast Guard would probably be able to do nothing more than posture and blather and then let them go.

When they finally pulled into the dock, it was clear that what the Coast Guard had found was no secret. There were almost 20 people there, a number of whom were clearly reporters and photographers from local media. But there were also people from Fish and Wildlife and the National Park service. Several of them carried side arms. This wasn't the welcome Karl had expected.

Once the animal was laid out on the dock and the people all gathered around, a woman came over to the wet sandy body to inspect it.

"I'm a veterinarian with the Miami Zoo." She explained. "The Coast Guard helicoptered me over here to look at this animal."

It didn't take her long. She examined the fur, looked at the eyes and teeth and found the entrance wound. She ran her hand along the animal's side and stopped just behind its heart.

"This animal had been starving. I don't think I've ever seen an animal this malnourished before. He was so close to death, your shooting him probably was a gift. That still doesn't make it right."

Karl guessed by then that even with everyone he knew in the political world, he would never retrieve the head, the pelt and those pricey genitals. At least he'd be paid by the governor and the ranch.

Ed, however, was pretty sure he was about to lose his boat and face a firestorm of bad publicity.

42

Drones were everywhere. Drive Alligator Alley, the Tamiami Trail or any road bordering the Everglades, Big Cypress and connected wetlands, and all you saw in the air were quadcopters and all sorts of other drones controlled by guys standing by their cars holding remotes. Luckily, the park service and Florida Wildlife jumped on this wave of public interest in finding tigers as soon as it formed. They set up a website where anyone with "interesting pictures or video" could post their images along with GPS coordinates of where they were taken. They named the site "panther-t." They were being inundated with images and video after only two days online.

Armed with the description of the putative trails in the grass described by Jake and Steve and photographed by Kim, rangers trained up a small army of volunteers quickly to scour the images and pick the most likely candidates for ones showing trails. The images had to have enough GPS information with them as well as time and date to make them useful to the data pool.

Many of the best images were sent to Randy at Flamingo. In just a couple of days he had developed a routine of waiting for everyone to leave the main building in the evening and then going into the offices with Tonya where he could access the park's best computers to analyze the pictures himself. Tonya didn't seem to mind being inside as long as she could be near Randy, and he appreciated the company even if conversation was mainly one-sided.

Personal drones have to be controlled from close proximity so their use was going to be limited to the periphery of the park, since the interior was still off limits to the public. Luckily both the state and federal government had been working together to get the military to share some of their images from high-resolution satellites. They had quickly found that public access satellite images just weren't good enough for finding trails in the grass or tigers on the ground. The first of these were promised to arrive at Randy's computer sometime within the next day or two.

The rest of the group at Flamingo had tried to continue the nightly ritual of a campfire and conversation with drinks whenever the late-day summer thunderstorms permitted. Only once so far did it include s'mores. By now even Shelly was getting used to, if not loving, the heat and humidity and the mosquitos and no-see-ums. This group had continued to use the pontoon boat to explore further up into the Glades, so they had plenty to talk about.

Jake and Steve knew that sooner or later they would have to have boots on the trails and even some wading in the waters to get the data they needed. They were holding off telling the others because it was likely no one else would like the idea of stalking tigers on foot, and there might even be open rebellion to stalking tigers while wading in the Glades waist deep in alligator and moccasin rich waters. And nobody had brought up the python issue lately, either.

The second night they were able to gather at the campfire, Kim drew out Saul's story, as promised. She didn't let him forget that he was on for that once they were settled in their camp chairs and were well into their evening libations.

"OK, OK,'" said Saul. He thought it was only fair to share his history since Kim had told her tale and he was basically interviewing everyone else constantly about their background and their work for the articles he planned to write.

"So skip the 'I was born at a very young age' part and get to the interesting stuff, Saul," Steve prompted.

"I don't know that any of it is interesting but you asked for it. Born and raised in the Big Apple on the Upper East Side. You know, son of privilege, meaning long trips to Florida in the winter with the family.

"Got to the beach whenever I could on those trips and became less and less satisfied with being in the city all the time. By the time I got to college, I was ready for some real rural. Went to Bowdoin, speaking of rural, and majored in English. I joined a frat there where the brothers were all the outdoorsy types. Skiing, snowshoeing, hiking; you know, like that. I loved it."

Randy could truly relate. He did miss Maine and his family right then.

"What I discovered was I wasn't so good at poetry and fiction writing," Saul continued. "What I really liked was writing about my minor, which was Environmental Studies. The professors thought I was OK at that, too, so that became my focus. I wrote those kinds of features for the school paper and even submitted some free-lance pieces to some national publications. A couple got published by my senior year."

"In spite of claiming to love all things outdoorsy, you seem really uncomfortable with being around Tonya, Saul. Why is that?" asked Steve.

"Uh, she's a tiger, man. They aren't known for their suitability as house pets and their 'great with children' demeanor. I'm just surprised you all are so calm around her. Besides, I spent lots of outdoor time in Maine being sure to stay out of the way of large animals like moose and bears. Call me crazy.

"So, anyway I got an internship at the "Sun Times" not long after college and stayed on when they offered me the job of writing obits. I did my best to get involved with the guy who was their environmental writer and eventually got out on a few stories with him. After a couple of years, they even let me write an article with him.

"All along I was doing some free-lance work, trying to hone my writing and make a little extra under the radar. When I started following the Army Corps of Engineers projects diverting water from the Glades for Miami and got some sources to give me information no one else had, I was able to convince my editors to put me on the environmental desk full time. That was when the guy I was apprenticing with there was just about to retire. So the rest is history, as they say. Told you it wasn't that interesting."

"Well your story didn't put me to sleep yet, so I'm still up for another round of drinks if the well isn't dry yet," said Shelly.

"Maybe its Tonya's turn next time to tell her story," joked Randy.

"Nothing like a good cat tale in a swamp," Shelly commented.

43

When the necropsy report from the tiger Messer shot the 10,000 Islands came through on the Internet, everyone at Flamingo was surprised. That animal was emaciated and filled with parasites. It had been dying for a long time and mostly without food in spite of killing two people. The vet had written that the parasites were likely from scavenging dead fish and other seafood and spending too much time totally wet in the islands' environment. Apparently either that animal didn't know how to hunt, which seemed unlikely considering his actions with Al and Mike, or there just wasn't enough suitable food available to hunt where he had been dropped off. She thought the animal had lost at least a third of its original body weight by the time it was shot. That didn't seem to be the story at all for Tonya.

When Randy had found her, she was hungry but in good condition. Her coat was still sleek and she didn't look the worse for being out in the Glades for however long she had been there. When he looked back at early reports, Randy thought that she had been sighted several weeks earlier by some tourists. But like all the other reports back then, that sighting was ignored.

If she had indeed been out there that long, she had to have been finding food and staying dry and out of parasite ridden areas for most of that time.

Actually, Tonya had been sold at birth to a guy in South Miami who just wanted the most exotic pet he could find. Tonya's mother was a captive in an unlicensed animal park in South Carolina and had been bred just so the park owners could sell the cubs and make enough money to keep from going bankrupt.

She had been raised in a small one-bedroom apartment and only rarely got to go outside. That happened in the middle of the night and well away from eyes that could see her and her owner. The good news was that her owner really grew to love this cat, and she grew to be far more docile than her species is usually known to be. The guy played all the usual cat games with her when they were together, so she learned to catch fast moving objects and hunt quietly.

When Tonya's owner lost his job due to the economic downturn, she got used to long days with him at home with her, but also to a lower quality of food. After about a month of that, her owner realized that he was not going to get employment any time soon and that he could not support Tonya much longer at any level. He had heard rumors that the Everglades had an environment similar to what some tigers were used to - full of good tiger food and fresh water. So he decided to find a way to get her deep in the Glades where she could be on her own and hopefully able to take care of herself. He really loved this cat but he didn't want to go to jail, which surely would have been the outcome had he tried to turn her over to animal rescue.

He borrowed a truck from a neighbor and found a way into the road to Flamingo well after dark, somehow getting around park security. About half way along that road he got Tonya out of the truck, hugged her hard with tears in his eyes and got back in the truck. Tonya was confused but didn't try to get back in the truck herself. When he pulled away she tried to follow but soon gave up after the taillights disappeared. She was alone for the first time in her life in a place she had never been before and knew nothing about. It would take her the better part of a week to find ways to keep herself alive and well, but she did it.

She tried several times to approach people who came into or out of the park, but either they never saw her or they moved off quickly. When Randy stopped and offered some food she recognized from her former life, she felt like this might be how she could get back to a more "normal" life. Ever since she had teamed up with Randy, Tonya had been comfortable and relaxed. She was outside a lot more than she had been in Miami; she had great food to eat and a good companion to play with. What more could a tiger want?

44

Karl Messer had made his way to the Keys after the ordeal with the authorities in Naples. God, what a nuisance that had been. He had to use every bit of pull he could to keep his freedom and his weapons without implicating the governor in any of it. It was almost easier dealing with the dickheads in Texas than it was with the assholes in Florida. He had to think hard to remember anywhere where he had been put through more nonsense than here. The closest he came was a big game hunt for gorillas he organized for some wealthy movie people from L.A. in Rwanda two decades ago.

He settled on a week-long rental of a 22-foot Grand Bay from Bump and Jump rentals on the Islamorada Key right after he killed two pints of beer and a big steak at Ziggy and Mad Dog's. He planned to get to the Flamingo area even with the park closed, and he knew he could do it by just crossing Florida Bay in the dark. He would take over finding the tigers from there and take them out. With any luck he could get some heads, some pelts and some organs and make some good money as well as get the governor some of that good press he wanted.

Karl didn't worry about the people at the park headquarters. He hadn't decided yet whether to skirt them entirely and pull up between Gibby Point and Porpoise Point east of Snake Bight and camp or just pull into the marina at the center and try to charm his way into the place. After another beer he figured the former course was the better option. He rented a kayak, a motorbike good for cross-country, and camping equipment. He spent the rest of the early evening rigging the bike so he could carry his arsenal with him. He would have to spend the next day provisioning himself and figuring how he could get the bike and his gear on the boat without raising suspicion and then get himself out on the water and out of sight as quietly as possible.

This was all good stuff as far as Karl was concerned. No reports to write and no clients to please. Just him, the tigers and the Glades. He was psyched!

45

"I never dreamed that a mere physical experience such as this could be so stimulating, Mr. Allnutt," Shelly/Hepburn said in a breathy voice as she stepped onto the pontoon boat.

"You mean you want us to go on with this trip, Rosie?" Jake/Bogart responded.

"I do indeed, Mr. Allnutt. And may I try steering a bit this time, sir?"

"You certainly may give it a try, old girl."

By now everyone in the marina was smiling again and trying to remember if these were real lines from "The African Queen" or just two fans of the movie really getting into the roles. It was certainly one of the best team building things going on with this group, rivalled only by the periodic "Kumbaya" campfire evenings when the weather permitted.

Today there were two pontoon boats going out. One would have Jake, Shelly and Kim, who would travel to the far side of Coot Bay and through the canal to the Midway Keys wetlands.

The other would carry Steve and Saul and two kayaks to navigate the mangrove tunnels and creeks between Coot Bay and Mud Lake and, if time permitted, between Mud Lake and Bear Lake. While Saul was slowly coming to terms with Tonya, he was very pleased when Randy declined Steve's invitation to join them. Randy had just been sent a file with some high-resolution satellite images and military drone pictures to analyze and he couldn't wait to get to it. He and Tonya were already back at headquarters booting up the computers for a few hours of image analysis.

Coolers full of water and food were loaded on each bigger boat along with a good supply of insect repellent, sunscreen, collecting equipment, machetes and, in the case of Jake and Steve, a serious weapon.

Shelly was certain Jake had only one outfit. It seemed as if the only clothes she had ever seen him in were the safari shirt and cargo pants. They always looked clean at the start of the day and the man didn't smell like he hadn't changed but you certainly couldn't count the passing days by a change in outfits. Only the sweat stain on the drover's hat hinted that it might be the one item that had probably not been changed out. Today Jake had the .44 magnum in a holster on his hip. Shelly was neither impressed nor comforted by that little number.

Kim had her bag of cameras and lenses. Whatever was found today would be well recorded in pictures. She even had a small video camera, although she didn't expect to be using it. The humidity was a concern and the fear of getting all of this equipment wet should something happen put her a bit on edge. She did have a rather cheap underwater camera with her, but she hoped she would never have to use that.

Since Steve and Saul were really not worried about scaring off animals until they were in the side creeks and in kayaks which would be quiet enough, their boat had only the standard twin outboards. Jake, Shelly and Kim were going to stay on the big boat and wanted to stay as quiet as possible when they got to the new bodies of water they were exploring, so they brought along a small electric motor for the front of the boat. It wouldn't move it fast but it would move it quietly.

Once everything was loaded, they headed up the canal in tandem. When they were about even with the mangrove creek between Coot Bay and Mud Lake, Steve peeled off to the west. He and Saul waved to the others, who stayed on course to the north.

When Steve anchored their boat in the shallows near the entrance to the creek that would take them to Mud Lake and shut off the engines, the first thing both he and Saul noticed was the profound silence. No generators, air conditioners, electric motors of any kind. No airplanes overhead either. Steve remembered this kind of silence from years ago when he was out here in the field far more often, but this was new for Saul. While he had spent time outdoors, there had always been the sounds of humanity and civilization somewhere close by. This was amazing. He wanted to write down this experience while he was living it, but as soon as he got out his notebook and pencil he found himself at a loss for words to describe what he was experiencing. It was amazing and somehow uncomfortable at the same time. Not even a breeze rustled the leaves on the mangroves.

Finally Saul broke the silence. "No birds."

"I see," said Steve. "Maybe we're in the wrong place for them. Or maybe the pythons have had more of an effect out here than we even thought. I don't know, but it's not comforting.

"Let's get the kayaks off this thing and start into the creek and see what we find."

They slipped the kayaks off the deck and tied them to the rail while they geared up. When they got into them, each carried water, some snacks, repellent, and a machete. Saul had his notebook and pencil, and Steve had his rifle, some extra ammunition and some sampling equipment. It seemed like a lot to carry for a day out on the water, but it was all necessary.

They untied and pulled away, paddling silently into the creek. The mangrove canopy seemed magical to Saul. He was hot and uncomfortable but had you asked him, he wouldn't have even been able to tell you that. Every so often, they had to lie back flat and bring the paddles horizontal along the boat to slip under the limbs.

Nothing along the route looked out of the ordinary or unexpected to either of them. When they broke out into Mud Lake, the flat calm surface of the water spread out in front of them, broken here and there by low islands covered in scrubby vegetation.

By now both men were perspiring profusely and the silence they had experienced at the start of this trip was now broken by the incessant whine of the hordes of mosquitoes buzzing around their heads and sweat-stained shirts.

"So much for the beauty of nature," thought Saul as he took a long pull on his water bottle. And now the sun was hammering down on them as well. "Maybe I should have gone with Kim," he thought. "At least their boat has a top and shade. It's bound to be more comfortable."

But Kim, Shelly and Jake were in the same river of grass and the shade didn't help all that much.

46

"The son of a bitch didn't tell them I'd hired him did he?" growled the governor.

"It appears not," his aide said. "It also seems like the kid he hired to get him into the Glades is keeping you out of it, too. We think he's hoping you'll find a way for him to get his boat back."

"Well he better not let this all get out of hand. I don't want any bad publicity for us coming out of this. It's all supposed to be good, right?"

"That's what we're working on, sir."

"So what's he up to now? Gone back to Texas?"

"He didn't really tell us where he was headed after he got free of all the authorities down there, so I took the liberty of calling the guys at the ranch to see if he had talked to them. He hadn't. No one knows where Messer is, sir, or what he's up to now, but everyone thinks he got scared off the tiger business by the response to his first kill. I'll let you know whatever we hear as soon as we hear it."

"OK then. See what you can do under the radar about the kid and his boat. And I guess we better get some state parks closed and get some positive press for doing our best to protect the public."

"I think the parks and rec people have already done that, sir."

"I couldn't care less. Find a way to position it so it was my idea or my order or something. I don't want those simpleton environmentalists to get credit when I should be the one getting it."

"Will do, sir. And your next appointment is with the sugar lobby. They have some proposals about what to do with some of the park land and maybe the Glades if it closes down the road."

"Well send them in, sister. They usually bring some really good liquor with them so get us some clean glasses and some ice. I'm lookin' for a long good afternoon with these boys."

"You want the Waterford glasses, Governor?"

"What else?"

47

Jake maneuvered the boat as close to the small island hammock as he could, but he knew that when he got close it was his turn to get wet if he was going to explore the place on foot. He figured the water was only about waist deep and he would have to wade ashore.

"Either of you two want to come along?" he asked, pointing to the island and preparing to go overboard.

"Uh, I think it might smear my nail polish so probably not a good idea," replied Shelly.

"I've got long lenses so I can capture 'Jake's Wonderful Adventure' from here, thanks," said Kim.

"Wimps!"

Jake took off his holster and gun and laid them on the deck near Shelly.

"Ever fire one of these?"

"No, but my dad used to watch a lot of westerns on TV so I know what it is at least," Shelly said.

"Well the safety is off and it's ready to go if anything goes wrong. The idea would be to shoot whatever is causing me a problem rather than just trying to put me out of my misery if you know what I mean. I don't expect any issues though. I just want to have a quick peek around and collect a sample or two if I find something and then wade on back here. Keep the boat steady if she moves at all."

"Aye, aye, Mr. Allnutt."

Jake slipped over the side and found himself a little deeper than he expected. His armpits were in danger of being really damp and not just from sweat. He waded slowly toward the shore of the small hammock sliding his feet on the bottom to scare any critters lurking on the bottom and feeling for obstacles to his progress. When he was about two feet from shore and about ready to step out on to land he reported, "Just bumped into something under water here. Feels like a log. Not what I would expect."

Having turned back to the boat to talk to Shelly and Kim he didn't see the "log" rise out of the water and move to coil around his waist and arms. Before he could react the "log" had him surrounded and was continuing to coil around his body.

"Oh, Christ no!" he yelled.

He fell into the water with the weight and motion of the twining "log" and gasped as the coils began to tighten around him, squeezing the air out of his chest. One coil was about mid chest and the whole mass seemed to be bringing him down and dragging him to where he would be under water in a matter of seconds.

Shelly seemed frozen in place watching as Jake was being squeezed and dragged along unable to fight off this thing.

"Python!" yelled Kim grabbing her camera and starting to take pictures in rapid fire succession.

Shelly dove for the gun and struggled to get it out of the holster not knowing there a hammer loop that kept it securely in place. Once she had it out though the bigger problem presented itself. Where to shoot or whether to shoot at all.

By now Jake was fully under water. Kim kept her camera firing away and not moving to help Jake or Shelly in any way. "Why the hell was she not helping?" thought Shelly.

Just then Kim yelled, "Behind him just on the shore!"

Shelly's head snapped around to see a huge reptilian head rise up off the dry shore and begin to move toward the coils now sinking back into the water where Jake had disappeared. Almost without thinking Shelly pointed the gun at the snake's huge head and pulled the trigger.

The sound was deafening but the kick of the gun is what Shelly noticed most. It felt as if her arm had just been blown off. She hurt everywhere. But when she looked, the snake's head was no longer attached to the end of its body and the coils that were visible seemed to be writhing randomly.

Shelly didn't realize that the weapon had flown out of her hand, but she just reacted and jumped into the water and started to pull the coils away from where Jake's body was last seen.

Kim had taken a few last shots, put down her camera and jumped in behind Shelly. Together they fought off the death throes of the python, untangled Jake and dragged him to shore. He was unconscious but they hoped still alive. They got his head and torso on land but left his legs floating in the water.

"What do we do now?" Shelly cried.

"Is he breathing at all?" Kim asked.

"Shelly put her ear close to Jake's mouth and nose and listened. She more felt a breath than heard it but she knew he was breathing and there weren't any sounds of water in the airway.

"Yeah, but very shallowly and not very fast."

"Well let's give it a few minutes and see if he recovers on his own. He's not blue. We can call for some help if we can get a cell phone signal out here."

It seemed like years rather than the seconds it took for Jake to begin trying to breathe more deeply. Every breath came with a groan of real pain. He didn't move much but at least he was breathing and mobile half out of the water.

"Go back on the boat and find a phone and try to get someone. I'll stay here and see what I can do to help Jake," said Kim.

"So now she does something positive," thought Shelly, bristling at being told what to do by someone who had just stood there taking pictures in the middle of the crisis.

Shelly moved around the still writhing coils of what was left of the python to get back to the boat. She guessed the animal was at least 12 feet long and probably longer.

When she hoisted herself onto the boat, she had to think hard about where she had put her phone. She saw the gun lying on the deck a good eight feet from where she had fired it and had no recollection of how it could have gotten that far away.

She gazed around the boat partly in shock and saw the bag she had brought aboard. Her phone was probably in there. When she got it out she just stared at the screen wondering if 911 had any meaning in the middle of the Everglades. She gave it a try anyway.

By now Jake's eyes were open and he was conscious. Very conscious of how hard it was to breathe and how much pain he felt all over his body.

48

"Tonya, my girl, no one is going to like this," Randy declared after about two hours looking over images he had been sent to analyze for evidence of tigers. The images were from a very high resolution photography satellite used for military surveillance. Randy had been looking for the kind of disturbances to the sawgrass or to vegetation along the edges between water and land that Steve and Jake had thought were not caused by natural native animal activity. He had images from a wide swath of the

Glades but he decided to focus his attention first on the area closest to Flamingo and work his way out from there.

If the disturbed grasses and vegetation of the magnitude he was looking at were really caused by tigers, the amount of tiger activity he was seeing was incredible. He was certain all of that activity couldn't be caused by just one tiger. Besides, he remembered Jake and Mike telling him of the sound recordings that the Cornell people had said belonged to two animals in close proximity to their campsite in Flamingo.

Randy really had only looked at about an area less than two square kilometers but he had already found enough evidence of tiger activity to suspect maybe as many as three or four animals in that region. That was way more dense than anything he had ever heard or read about in wild tiger populations. If this was real, he could be looking at a disaster in the making both for the Glades and the tigers themselves, which would all be competing for limited space and food. That didn't even take into consideration how much pressure they would put on other animals that overlapped their niche.

Time to call others looking at images to see what they were finding and get some more guidance.

"Hey Shark Valley, this is Randy down at Flamingo. I wanted to check into see if your people looking at aerial and satellite images are finding anything up your way?"

"Why do you ask?" replied Paul from the Shark Valley analysis team.

"I just want to see if we are both on the same track with this."

"What have you found in this short a time?"

"I guess I asked you first and I'd rather not bias your response by saying what I've been finding, OK?"

"OK, I guess. We've looked at drone shots from aerial surveys done along the Shark Valley trail here and we have seen pushed down grass trails in more places than we thought we would. There's enough of them to make us suspect that if they are caused by tigers as your people suggested, we probably have quite a few more than we would have expected."

"Any preliminary estimate to the density based on what you've seen so far?"

"We're guessing, mind you, from very little area covered so far and lots of ifs, but if we were pressed we'd say probably about two to four animals in a three to four square kilometer area. So what have you got so far?"

"Sorry to report exactly the same probable conclusion. I just hope that when the people get back here from the field they bring us some alternative explanation for what we're looking at. I don't think anyone would want what we are estimating to be true."

"Right with you on that. We're back at it on the drone pix for a day or so more and then on to some satellite images. Keep going and stay in touch with what you find."

"Will do, Paul."

Randy turned to Tonya, gave her head a pat and said, "Time for a snack and some outside time and then we're back at it girl. You with me?"

He could almost convince himself he saw her grin when the word snack was mentioned. As he got up to get their food he heard a helicopter overhead and rushed to a window to see a Coast Guard rescue helicopter flying low and heading up the trail where the two boats that had left in the morning had gone. Not the best sign.

49

"Not more goddamn Coast Guard," thought Karl as he watched the copter buzz low over his campsite. He had gotten to the beach before dawn and set up just enough to catch some z's before off-loading the boat and getting really set up. He had sung himself to sleep with the soothing tunes of Jack Daniels. Probably should have been Charlie Daniels but Jack was much quieter. That had made for a good sound sleep until that orange striped mosquito flew over.

"How the hell did they find out I was here?" he thought to himself. "And if they did find out, why didn't they see me and come right back?"

Karl went ahead and fixed his "morning" coffee and waited for the troops to arrive. No sense in waiting with a hangover in this heat if you can kill it with caffeine. But they never came.

He guessed that they had been after something else in the Glades, maybe aerial surveys for the tigers or something, and he had gotten it wrong that they knew he was there. "Good for Karl!" he thought. Time to get on with it.

He moved everything back away from the water's edge and tucked what he could under vegetation making it hard for anyone to see his setup from the air. Just in case they came back later. He wolfed down some jerky and a couple of biscuits before setting off in his camo inflatable kayak along the shore to reconnoiter. Damn surplus store only had desert camo inflatables though. Who the hell would think about kayaking in a desert? Oh, wait. The Army. What had he been thinking?

The rifle was only 10 pounds and the handgun was five, so he wasn't laden with too much weight but still felt well-armed. A half-gallon of drinking water and he was good to go.

He didn't want to get too close to the visitor center where he might be seen but he did want to survey the shoreline close to there and then well east of his campsite as well. It wouldn't take him that long to get the lay of the land from the water view and the map he had studied before coming here. Once he was back at the camp, he could take some short walks inland to see how much access he had from where he was and how well he could stay out of sight.

Karl was a very happy hunter at this point. He knew there were tigers out there to be had. He had killed one already, hadn't he? He had skills for staying unseen and living out here for days without any contact with others. This was way better than shepherding clueless clients around in a Land Rover in order to shoot some zoo animal for a trophy head just because it was legal.

By dusk Karl was set to go. Tomorrow he would set off to find some trophies for himself and maybe get the governor the good kill he had wanted in the first place.

50

Steve and Saul got back on their pontoon boat and stowed the kayaks for the trip back to the visitor center. They were whipped from the humidity and heat and disturbed by the silence that surrounded them. Other than insects, what animals were still alive out here? Hard to tell from what they had seen and heard. The few sounds they made out could have been wind, limbs snapping on a hammock or their imagination.

"You know Steve, as I recall, Jake and his student recorded some sounds that were i.d.'d as tiger a while back. I don't think any of us has heard anything like that since then. I would have expected that if there are tigers out here, somebody would have heard something again by now. Not all this silence."

"Yeah, I agree. It's strange. Too quiet for my tastes. It's not what I remember from my field days out here but to tell the truth, I wasn't out here hardly at all this time of year. Heat, humidity, and storms just made being inside seem better, even back then."

"Let's use the electric motor more on the way back so we can hear anything that is making noise out there."

"OK. Why don't you get your cell phone ready to record anything if any sound comes our way? Who knows, we might even record that Ivory-billed Woodpecker everyone knows is extinct."

"How good are you at imitating animal sounds? You could always give a friendly roar and see if you get an answer."

"I'll pass on that one. Thanks anyway."

They set off back toward "home" with just enough speed to have a slight breeze blow past them. Not a sound came their way the whole way back.

51

Shelly and Kim stood at the shore of the little island and watched as the Coast Guard rescuer signaled the helicopter crew to reel in the basket with Jake strapped in it and him holding onto the cable from which it was suspended. They followed the two up to the opening in the side of the deafening machine and waited until it lifted slightly, dipped to one side and flew away to the east.

As silence began to overtake them again, neither woman seemed able to move. Trauma can paralyze you and make you numb. Just what they were both feeling at the moment.

After a few minutes that actually seemed like hours, they made their way through the water back to the pontoon boat, avoiding the remains of the python still visible next to the island. They scrambled aboard and sat, both breathing hard, more from adrenalin than exertion.

Kim moved first and got the motors going slowly. She backed the boat away from the island and got it started toward the visitor center. Shelly still hadn't moved much. Kim picked up Jake's gun with two fingers and slid it back in the holster, leaving both on the deck of the boat.

Once they had been underway long enough to get some breeze blowing in their faces for resuscitation, Shelly began to massage the hand and shoulder that had held and fired the gun. When she was more recovered she couldn't help herself from challenging Kim.

"What the hell were you doing back there, woman!

"That snake was all over Jake and all I saw you do was snap pictures. It's no wonder you people have such a bad reputation. The almighty picture comes before helping someone stay alive. I never figured you for a card-carrying paparazzi!"

Strangely, Kim didn't react as if she had been slapped, the reaction Shelly had expected and hoped for. She just sat down and sighed. She wasn't sure she should defend herself but she had been over this territory so many times in her own mind, now seemed as good a time as any to voice it to someone else.

"I know the reputation of some media photogs, and believe me I know that reputation is well deserved," she began in a quiet voice.

"In spite of what you think right now, that's not what I am or ever have been. My taking pictures back there had nothing to do with putting photographs before someone's life or safety."

"Hard to believe from what I saw!" Shelly retorted.

"One of the sad truths for people in our business is that we are sometimes put in situations that are dangerous to others and even ourselves. What we have to do in split seconds then is decide whether we will be able to help a situation by throwing down the camera and rushing toward that danger or whether doing that might actually make the situation worse."

"So you thought taking pictures was going to help Jake more than going after the gun or trying to help get that thing off of him?" Shelly asked incredulous.

"Not taking pictures, Shelly, just any action I might have taken then. I don't know how to use a gun, Jake showed you how. I would have just as likely shot him as the snake had I tried to use it." All the while Kim's voice was calm but neither condescending nor contrite.

"Why not get over there to start dragging the thing off him then?" Shelly countered.

"I could tell in a heartbeat that the snake was way too strong for even the two of us to wrestle. If I had jumped in there I could have easily either distracted you or been right in your line of fire and kept you from acting before it was too late."

"You still had the where-with-all to keep the shutter clicking though, didn't you?"

"That's the reflex of a photojournalist. It also means that sometimes we get images that tell the story of an incident better than the narratives people in the middle of a situation develop after the fact. And sometimes one of those images makes a big difference in how a lot of people see situations."

Shelly sat silently for a while, starting to see what Kim was trying to tell her.

"Think back to some of the most iconic images of dangerous situations and how they led to people understanding what was going on. The dead and dying on battlefields from Brady's Civil War pictures, up through the wars going on today. The lone man standing up to a row of tanks. The little girl running naked away from her napalmed village. The blood bath of The Cove. And on and on. They were all taken by people who couldn't make a positive difference in the moment but they could make images that might make a difference down the road. That's what we hope for in those situations even though we know it won't happen the vast majority of the time or for most of us in the business. That's why I kept taking pictures."

With that Kim slumped and let the fear she had felt all along come to the surface. She began to cry softly.

Shelly wasn't sure she bought it all but she certainly understood Kim better than she had when they stepped off that island. And right now, as sweaty and slimy as they both were, Shelly knew that embracing Kim and holding her close was the right thing to do for both of them.

52

"Not as much Kumbaya tonight with jungle man up in Miami," noted Shelly as they sat out around a small smoky fire.

"True, but it was good to hear that his ribs are just badly bruised and not broken. They did say he should be back here tomorrow so we can break out the sing-along sheets and play-along instruments then," Kim replied.

Saul had been getting increasingly comfortable with Tonya and was now even sitting more or less beside her tonight. Even so, he left a good bit more room between himself and the tiger than he did between him and Steve on his left.

Once everyone had heard the story of Jake and the python as told by Shelly and Kim, and the phone call had come in about Jake's condition from the hospital up in Miami, debriefing the day's work began.

Randy was so excited he didn't even wait to be asked first to tell his news. Probable tigers everywhere. Every analyst on the images reported the evidence. Not what anyone had hoped for. He passed around some of the pictures he had enhanced for analysis so everyone around the campfire could see what he and the other analysts had seen. Once he summarized his numbers and what they most probably meant, conversation did not come easily.

Steve and Saul talked a bit about the stillness they had found but made their story short since it didn't seem to add anything new and certainly was not nearly as dramatic as Shelly and Kim's or as sobering as Randy's. In fact the whole day had been a sobering experience all around. Silence fell over the group as everyone just stared into the flames, immersed in their own thoughts and processing the day's news. No one made a move to head into the campers. And no one had anything more to say.

As the fire died to embers a muffled rumble reached the group. It was from far off to the north. It certainly wasn't thunder. They all looked up simultaneously and stared at each other acknowledging the sound. Steve just shook his head slowly and stood silently, inviting them all to head inside.

53

Karl had done some homework, not his forte but necessary for this job. He had found that tigers make a kill on average every eight or nine days and eat 40 or more pounds of food from each kill at one time. He had come prepared to lure his quarry with food. The people who had sold him the 200 pounds of horse meat didn't show the slightest bit of interest in why he wanted it. They threw in some dry ice to help him transport it, though.

Since he had night vision binoculars and a night vision scope on his rifle, Karl thought he'd try his luck this first night by letting a good hunk of the meat warm to swamp temperature and then putting it out in a fairly open area well up the path into the Glades from his camp. He had scouted out just the spot and

124

a way to get up into the vegetation enough to be well above the bait. Not quite a tree stand like he was used to for deer hunting, but good enough.

He had chilled some of that good whiskey he had brought with him in the dry ice and put it in a thermos. He had a canteen for water but who needs water when you're just sitting in a blind waiting?

He had no idea that others had tried baiting the tigers to minimal avail elsewhere, so his expectations were higher than they probably should have been.

You would have thought that putting away one thermos of whiskey over a three hour period wouldn't have affected someone like Karl quite so much. But he had fallen asleep. When he woke up, light was just beginning to brighten the area around him. Looking down at the spot where he had put the meat before climbing to his current position, he couldn't really make it out very well.

When he got to the site, he found the meat gone. There didn't seem to be any evidence of what might have taken it while he was asleep. It was too far from water to have been a gator or a croc. It could have been a bear. Even more unlikely it could have been a panther. After a quick look around he picked up his gear and headed back to camp to think what to do next. Had he known what to look for and where to look, Karl would have noticed an orangish clump of coarse hair, almost hidden by a leaf, stuck to a low branch of a small shrub beside the trail.

54

Jake was back and hurting but not complaining much. He made his way gingerly over to the conference room for the meeting.

With all the confirmations of probable tigers in the Glades it was time once again for a meeting to develop an action plan. The super decided to hold the meeting at Flamingo, out of direct public access, so they could plan without the crazies disrupting the proceedings. The main administrators and key personnel had made their way to Flamingo for the afternoon meeting. Most had been nervous about that loose tiger wandering around the area with that young guy but they soon got over it once they had met them both face to face.

While it was really the superintendent's meeting, he had deferred to Steve to run it since he knew everybody involved and had been on the problem from the beginning. Jake sat in the back close to a door where he could quietly escape if the discomfort got to be too much for him. Randy and Tonya sat beside him out of sight of most participants so as to be less distraction.

"Thanks for making the effort to get down here for this meeting," Steve began. "If you don't already, you will soon all agree that we have a serious problem on our hands. It's not just about some people getting themselves killed in the park. As you all know that happens all the time in our world. It really is about a new invasive and this one is a doozy.

"In the past, invasives have been brought into regions in small numbers and have taken years to balloon into the serious problems they are. This one came on us like a bolt out of the blue, and it looks like it already is more of a problem than we could have predicted, even if we had known about it early on.

"During this meeting we'll go over a little tiger biology. Then we'll go over what we think we know about the problem of tigers in the Everglades and how we came to know it. Then we'll review several speculative scenarios about what might happen with this problem under a variety of circumstances. Finally we'll break out into groups to brainstorm possible action plans to remediate this problem.

"Once we have a few possible action plans on the table we'll prioritize those action plans. You'll be sent back in teams. Each team will explore one of those action plans and find ways to predict the likelihood of your team's plan succeeding. We'll meet again, probably here, in about four days with those reports and decide which of those plans we will try to implement from here. Any questions?"

"A lot of us know most of what you're going to bore us with in the early part of this meeting," began one of the head rangers. "Can we be excused from that part?"

"I'll let the super answer that one but from my own perspective it would probably be best if we all just sat through it all even if we have been through it before so we start this process all on the same page."

The superintendent stood and indicated his agreement with Steve. Either anxious to get going or already bored, the audience had no more questions.

Jake knew he was only going to make it through about half of this meeting and he really wanted to be in on the planning rather than listening to a rehash of information he already knew a lot about, so he told Randy he'd be back and slipped out and headed back to the camper to rest until the planning started.

55

"There seems to be a break in the action down in the Glades, sir," reported the governor's aide. "They haven't had a press conference in a while and there have been no reports about what's going on there, even on social media."

"Well that sounds better," the governor replied. "Let's hope that trend continues. Any word on that hunter from King Ranch? Did he ever get back to Texas?"

"No sir. Just dropped off the map as far as anyone can tell. The ranch isn't worried though. He's about the best they have. They'd just like him back or at least to report in."

"Any chance he could have been eaten out there?"

"Not likely sir. They say he's too good to let that happen. It's just nobody knows even where to start looking, so it's just wait 'til he calls in, I guess."

"So what's next on the calendar for today, kiddo?"

"It's the phosphate lobby, sir. They're here about help with the outcry about the newest sinkhole problem and something to do with mineral rights in that thing called the wildlife corridor or something. They say that you will be delighted to see them once you open this, sir."

The aide passed a manila envelop to the governor. He opened it slowly and read the sheet of paper he took out of it. A smile as wide as the Mississippi split his face.

"Send them in, son. And bring the good glasses with that whiskey the sugar people left."

Near the Cape Verde islands off the West Coast of Africa a small atmospheric depression was forming. It would have a chance to grow as it progressed westward along the trade winds because the sub-Saharan dust storms were not as strong as usual this year. The dust storms were being caused by drought coupled with excess farming in the Sahel region over the last decades. The result was that the desert expanded southward into the winds that blow across the Atlantic. Miami, among other places, had been plagued by the red dust they carried. Back in the late

1990s fungal spores carried in these soils had landed on the coral reefs around the Caribbean and Western Atlantic and had sickened and killed sea fans all across the region. This trend of increasing dust storms and their impact in the Western Hemisphere had generally continued. But this season, at least up until now, there had been only a few such storms, and those had been less severe than previous ones. That meant that the tropical sun in the Atlantic had been only minimally shielded by dust in the air. The surface of the Atlantic off of West Africa was hot. Perfect conditions to fuel the growth of a tropical depression.

56

Kim and Saul had trouble finding any story in the meeting at Flamingo and so asked their editor and the folks at Flamingo if they could take a few days in other parts of the park and beyond to expand their coverage. Everyone agreed that probably was a good idea. They found a ride to Miami with one of the departing meeting goers, rented a car and headed off to Shark Valley and beyond to get some perspective from there.

Once you tell the public it can't do something, a significant number will try to find ways to do it anyway. That is what happened at Shark Valley. People were coming from everywhere along the Tamiami Trail and Alligator Alley and slipping through any barriers the park service or anyone else had set up in order to get out into the Glades to look for tigers. Almost all of them had found insects, alligators and moccasins but no tigers. A few had even run across pythons. So far, none had an encounter like Jake's.

The few who claimed to have run across tigers or evidence that they were there had been lucky the cats had little interest in them as food although the rangers seemed to indicate tongue-in-cheek that they wouldn't have minded if a few of those idiots had seen one really close up and personal. So far, the work of looking for how far the problem extended was taking up most of everyone's time not devoted to chasing tiger tourists.

"The gang at Flamingo don't know how lucky they are being isolated from all the nut jobs. We're just too accessible to people for our own good," the superintendent told them during their stop at the visitor center.

"We're going to have another attack for sure if for no other reason than that we can't close the roads that get people out here. Early on, I couldn't even sleep from worrying about that. I'm about at the point of just suggesting to everyone who wants to come here to see a tiger, 'Come ahead but rub yourself down in Montreal seasoning before you go out there. You want to give them a tasty meal, don't you?'"

Kim and Saul left Shark Valley without any significant additions of narrative or images to their story so they set off to their next stop, Clyde Butcher's photo gallery. He was here at his place in Big Cypress rather than up at the one in Venice, so they had a chance to talk to him, his wife Niki and some of his staff who were still working in spite of the slowdown in tourist traffic and the tiger threat.

Kim had long been a fan of Butcher's work with large format cameras and black and white printing to capture the beauty of the environment, earning him the nickname "Ansel Adams of the Everglades." Kim never lost the thrill of standing in front of the huge prints of Big Cypress, the Glades or other natural beauty spots, letting herself dive into the images in all their telling clarity and detail. Saul had never been to Butcher's place. He was gob-stopped on arrival, first at the setting of the studio and second at the photographs that confronted him. He was delighted further to see Clyde's wife's hand-colored renderings that gave totally different vibes from the black and whites. It certainly didn't hurt that Clyde looks every part of the character he is from his hat to his shorts. His world could be a story in itself, and both Kim and Saul tucked that thought into the backs of their minds for a later date and another major feature article possibility.

Everyone there thought that they had caught a glimpse of a tiger or seen evidence of them since the first reports had surfaced. The studio had stopped doing photo safaris out back on the property, and no one walked to or from their cars alone. They even monitored the parking lot in case anyone who stopped happened to be alone. Then one of the staff would go out and escort them into the studio.

"I think I'm set to close up down here until things settle out a bit more and it feels safer for everyone. It just feels bad to have my people down here out of work for however long. We'll take care of 'em financially, of course, but most of them are here for the love of the place, Big Cypress and the Glades. It's going to be hard, let me tell you," Clyde told Kim and Saul. They thanked him for his time and his beautiful work and stepped outside. "Where to next writer-man?" Kim asked Saul as they headed to their car.

"Go west, young journalists." Saul suggested with a smile.

"Are you suggesting that big fish camp by the Ten Thousand Islands?"

"Well sure. Might just catch us some dinner as well as a couple of interviews," he replied.

"OK. But maybe we should stop for a bottle of tartar sauce on the way then. Whaddya think?"

57

Karl had been hearing things in the near distance every night when he was back at his camp. He had seen plenty of signs, but no animals. He even had spent the better part of one afternoon tracking a cat that had left some fresh prints in mud along a path going north into the Glades. He never caught up. What he failed to find was where the big animal had circled around and begun tracking him. For some reason it left his trail after a short time and headed toward a hammock to the East.

Karl wasn't sure why he needed to keep going after a kill but he was having more fun than he'd had since deployment. He loved the discomfort, the heat, the humidity, the being wet everywhere, the stink of rotting horse meat for bait and whole days with a gun in his hand. He'd deal with the moneymen when he got back. Luckily, he had brought enough booze with him to last quite a while out here, even at his rate of consumption.

Time to try the tree stand thing again, he thought. This time he had some places in mind where he had seen tiger signs, so he had more confidence in a better result. He also promised himself not to drink quite so much that he slept through most of the night like last time.

So after downing an MRE that he brought along from one of those military surplus stores, he dragged a piece of the stinking meat to his chosen location, smeared himself with some of the stench to cover his "human" smell, grabbed his gun and his bottle and climbed his tree as night fell.

Six hours and about half a quart later, he heard some crashing noise approaching his bait. He lowered his infra-reds and spotted a cat in the undergrowth slinking his way. He tried to position himself so he could take a sniper's steady pose assuring a one-shot kill. As he did the cat came out of hiding, grabbed the meat and started back into the vegetation. As Karl swept the gun toward a firing position the barrel smacked a limb, startling the cat, which held on to the meat and dashed back under cover before Karl had a chance to recover. He was so mad he let loose five quick shots into oblivion. Maybe he killed a lizard or shot off some limbs on some bushes but he didn't come close to the cat.

"Damn that felt good!" he said, happy enough to have shot at nothing just to feel the weapon buck in his hand and the explosions leaving his ears ringing. He took a long drag on what was left of his bottle, climbed down and headed back to camp, knowing he'd had his only chance for a tiger that night.

"More to come, man. More to come," he thought.

What Karl had missed in his self-created chaos was that the cat he was primed to kill that night was not a tiger but a Florida panther which was finding it hard to make a living in its native home because of all the strange new things trying to make a living. At least it would eat tonight.

58

Route 29 runs from near Gatorama at Fisheating Creek Preserve to Everglades City, inland of some of the most heavily populated Gulf Coast development in South Florida. It also runs through the National Wildlife Reserve for the Florida Panther, Big Cypress and the Everglades. There is little population along the road and little traffic, particularly in the off-season. The road is a prime location for speed and letting your attention wane while driving. Consequently it has become a killing field for panthers and other wildlife that venture onto its blacktop.

If you draw a triangle to Route 29 from Naples and Fort Myers you come very close to the Audubon property of Corkscrew Swamp and the town of Immokalee.

The Roosevelt family had just left Corkscrew where they had thought they would walk the trails after they had spent a morning stop at Gatorama for the kids. They found Corkscrew still closed so they had turned around and headed back to Route 29.

They had been on a short summer vacation trip just to get out of town for a day or so. Now they were on their way south, hoping to get back to their home in Plantation earlier than they had expected.

"Russ, you could slow down," remarked Laverne, Russ's wife.

"Hey, there's nobody on the road. Who cares how fast I go. We'll make it home sooner this way."

As he looked back down at his phone checking for any new messages, one of the kids in the back yelled, "Dad! Animal!"

Russ looked up just as the car grazed a blur of orange and black that had been racing to cross the road in front of them. The animal that was hit tumbled along the tarmac and the body came to rest on the gravel verge. It lay motionless. The car was partially turned around in the middle of the road.

"Anybody hurt here?" Russ asked.

"No, we're OK," everyone replied.

"I better check on the car," Russ said, opening the driver's side door.

"Don't go out there, Russ," Laverne said, her voice shaking from the shock of the crash.

"Hey, look," Russ replied. "The animal's not moving a muscle. Probably dead anyway. I gotta find out if this thing is drivable. And don't go calling anyone while I check. If we can drive, we're getting out of here before someone comes along and identifies us. That thing out there is one of them tigers we've heard about, and I just don't want us to get involved or fined or whatever they do if you go and hurt one of them."

With that Russ opened the door, stepped out of the car and went to the front where he could see the damage more clearly. The driver's side bumper, headlight and panel were just about destroyed. It didn't look like the left front tire was compromised from turning and there probably wasn't any damage to the engine. So Russ thought they could just drive away. As he was turning back to get into the car he heard his family screaming in unison. It was, unfortunately, the last thing that Russ Roosevelt ever heard.

59

"I could have sworn I heard some banging or some sort of manmade sound last night. It might have been part of a dream or something but I don't think so," Shelly said as they settled near the campfire ring for the evening wine and kibitz.

"Why maybe it was last night's wine talking, Rosie old girl," Jake came back in his best Bogart since the banter had begun.

"Mr. Allnutt, are you questioning my sobriety?" Shelly responded, falling immediately into her Hepburn voice.

"I hate to take sides here in the middle of Old Movie Night but I thought we heard something, too," Randy mentioned with his hand on the nape of Tonya's neck.

"Well I don't know of anyone other than us out here now and we certainly are well away from the crazies who are getting into the park everywhere else. If there is someone out here other than us, they certainly shouldn't be, and who knows why they are here. I think we need to act as if there are others we don't know about out here and be sure we are never out alone. And if Jake is OK with it, I think it's time Randy and Tonya spend their nights indoors, meaning Jake's place." Steve was aware he was being overly cautious but he also was sure he couldn't rely on the assumption that they were alone.

"It's OK with me," said Jake. "As long as Tonya doesn't try to sleep on my chest and break some of these bruised ribs, I'm fine with it."

60

"Bulletin, Governor," said the aide, bounding into the Governor's office. "Another kill down south."

"Immigrant or policeman?" asked the Governor.

"Neither," replied the aide. "Tiger."

"So someone finally shot another tiger out there?"

"Uh, no sir. A tiger killed a motorist on 29 north of all the swamps. Seems like they're expanding out of the Glades."

"So this tiger stops a car, maybe askin' for a ride, and instead of hopping in, kills the driver. Is that it? What actually happened son?"

"It seems this family from Plantation was on a short vacation trip and on their way home. The dad was driving when a cat jumped in front of their car and he hit it. He thought it was dead so he got out to see what damage he had on the car and the cat jumped up and took him away into the scrub. All they found were bits of clothes."

"How do they know it was a tiger that got him?"

"The family was still in the car and witnessed the whole thing. They're still pretty much beside themselves."

"Any comment from the national people?"

"No sir. Not yet anyway."

"What do our Fish and Wildlife people have to say?"

"They haven't said anything yet, either."

"Gee I wish you'd come in here with a lot less information. My head is rightfully swimming in data right now, from all you brought."

Whether the sarcasm was lost on the aide or not was unclear. All he could say was, "Yes sir,"

"Let's see what falls out of this one. Maybe it'll be the straw that breaks the back of those environmentalist types. One of these incidents sure should be. If that ever happens we'll finally be able to get on with the business of filling in those hell holes and get some good capital investment in that area rather than grass and gators. Keep me informed, but try to get some real detailed information before you come trotting in here again."

"I'm on it, sir"

"God damn, is that the only thing these people know how to say?" the Governor mumbled *sotto voce* as his aide slid out of the office.

Not quite strong enough to catch anyone's attention yet, the depression off the west coast of Africa was beginning to build. Sea temperatures in the area hovered around 30 degrees C, incredibly warm for the area. The buildup was still north of Cape Verde at about 20 degrees north. It would be one to watch, once anyone put it on their radar.

61

The journalists were headed next to Chokoloskee, the place where the whole problem first showed itself. Maybe there was more story out there than met the eye when they were at Flamingo. They both still felt the heart of anything they wound up reporting on would most likely center on the Flamingo team, but the story was expanding in their eyes, maybe faster than the tiger population.

"So before this gig, what was the best assignment you ever had?" Kim asked as she drove them toward Everglades City.

"That's kind of a tough one, Kim. I've had a lot of great assignments. I love the ones they send me on in the Keys. I got into diving after I took a free-lance job for a magazine on an Earthwatch project looking at bleaching and diseases on the coral reefs of the Bahamas. The diving has always been great, even when the subject I was writing about wasn't so positive. But to pick just one assignment that was the best, I guess I'd have to say the one I had for the paper on Isle Royale and the wolf and moose populations up there."

"Really? You like the cold, writer-man? I mean I seem to recall that project is done in the winter on an island in Lake Superior, right?"

"Yeah, it is and it is damn cold and primitive. I was out there something like three weeks, but the people running the project are out there seven."

"What was it that you liked so much?"

"I loved the place, the isolation, the wildness. I'd never been in such a wild place before. Then to see just how much these people were learning about how predators and prey interact was amazing."

"Like what?"

"You can't just look at how two species interact out there. Everything seems connected. Before the wolves made it to the Isle, the moose population had exploded and devastated a whole bunch of the plant species. Then they starved and their population dropped. Once the wolves got there, it looked like they would keep the moose populations under control, bringing back a healthier woodland and wetland. But then the populations of wolves exploded and it was boom/bust for a couple of decades. It turns out the wolves formed packs to keep ravens from eating too much of their food, so the whole interaction affected those populations, too. Then warmer than usual seasons brought on a tick infestation in the moose, and that affected everything in different ways.

"I can't help thinking the tiger issue in the Glades here is going to present us with some very complicated and maybe unpredictable changes in a whole bunch of parts of the system, just like Isle Royale has.

"Anyway, that's my story and I'm stickin' to it.

"Your turn – favorite assignment of all time."

"Easy for me to pick. I know you saw the story because we ran it not that long ago. We did a big feature on Genie Clark. She was known most of her career as 'The Shark Lady' for all the work she did on them all over the world. She had a big hand in forming Mote Marine Lab up in Sarasota. When we did the story she was in her 80s. Anyway, she was great to be around, really friendly and easy, and amazingly vital. She was headed out into the Gulf to dive with whale sharks to get more insights into their ecology. We got to go along for the week out there, and I got to film her work underwater and on board the research vessel. Food wasn't that good, but everything else was fantastic!

"Can't say what we learned there has as much bearing on the tiger issue here as yours, but based on your story, who knows."

"Cool, Kim. Since we're both divers maybe we could do some together once this is over. Maybe we could even find a dive-requiring story to do together."

"Might be fun."

As Kim was finishing her story, they made the turn by the big white old Collier County courthouse in Everglades City toward Chokoloskee. The narrow road to the island was deserted, as had been all the airboat tour and kayak concessions around Everglades City. As they pulled onto the island past the trailer park, they both had the feeling they were entering a ghost town. No one was out. They headed down to the Smallwood store and marina hoping to find some locals to interview and maybe even some food. Even ghosts have to eat sometime.

62

The team at Flamingo met in the conference room. Steve had just spent about an hour on the phone with the superintendent who was still up at Shark Valley.

"What's the urgency with this meeting, Steve?"

"I just got off the horn with the super. There's been another person killed by a tiger. This one is going to change how we look at this problem from here, though."

"How?" Jake asked.

"This one was out of the park."

"How far out of the park?" Randy asked.

"Up near Corkscrew."

"So what does that mean?" asked Shelly.

"It means either that the tigers from down here are on the move, expanding beyond the park, or people are still dumping their tigers, and since they can't get in here easily, they dump them somewhere that looks something like the Glades."

"How can we know which it is, Steve?" asked Jake.

Shelly jumped in before Steve had a chance to answer. "If I could get some DNA samples down here from outside the park, I can try to match them with some of the samples we've gotten before. They may not be from the same individuals, but we may find some relationships that show up in the sequences. If they're related, it could show the animals are moving. If not, it might mean that new drops are the source.

"Think you can get me some samples, Steve?"

"I wish I could say yes for sure, but this is the first confirmed animal outside the park. We have got to expand where we are looking. Then maybe we could track down some samples for you. We aren't the authority outside the park, so we'd have to rely on other agencies, mainly state. They've been seriously underfunded lately, so who knows what they'll be able to do for us."

"Can you get me new aerial or satellite images of the areas outside the park where these animals might be? I'll use what we know so far to look for evidence for them in those places," Randy said.

"We can certainly do that, but that could be a big area, Randy. If we use the pythons as a guide, they have spread to the counties surrounding the park, and the water districts out there have hired professionals to hunt them in their water resources. They're not finding many, even though they know there are thousands out there. And remember those guys just slither and swim along very slowly."

"Why would the tigers have moved north rather than say east into Miami?"

"My guess would be the wildlife corridor, Shelly." Jake answered. "We talked about that before."

"I know we did, Jake, but everyone said we would have heard about this a while ago if they were moving through there. So why now?"

"Your guess is as good as anyone's now, Shelly. We'll just have to see where this leads us."

"So Steve, does this mean that we are going to have to leave this paradise and create a traveling tiger search?" Shelly asked.

"No. In fact the super and I think we need to stay where we are so we can better control the information flow out of the survey. We are still worried about public overreaction, political fallout from all levels, and crazies from everywhere. We're still in the best position to avoid most of that down here.

"We may need to re-evaluate our living situations soon though."

"Hey, let's put Randy and Tonya in with Saul when he and Kim get back. That could be good for some evening entertainment." Shelly suggested.

"Well that's not exactly what I had in mind, but it could be fun.

"Actually, Randy has just told me about some evidence of tigers around Eco Pond Trail by the T lot. It wasn't Tonya that left it, either. That probably means some are moving our way, too. I think we need to think about how we can more limit our movements, particularly at night. We may eventually need for all of us to camp out in the main buildings or something like it. We'll talk more about that over the next day or so. In the meantime, be extra careful out there."

"Oh Goody! Dorm life returns to the wicked. I do refuse to eat the mystery meat in the cafeteria, though," Shelly joked.

"Why I had no idea you were such a *prima donna,* Rosie old girl," Bogart/Jake responded.

63

As Karl thought back to the tiger attacks he knew of, he realized that they had all taken place during the day. Here he was assuming his best chance for taking out a tiger would be at night. Maybe he needed a change of strategy. He had fought as a mercenary in hotter and more humid conditions than these, so slogging it out here in the heat of the day wasn't a deterrent.

His map showed a couple of trails that the park service stopped maintaining because of some endangered plant. They were still passable and could be connected by using the main park road. The trails were only about three or four miles from the visitor center but with no one in the park at the moment, he was fairly sure he would be alone out there.

So Karl prepared himself for the 15 mile hike from his camp and around the Snake Bight and Rowdy Bend Trails. No booze this time. He would wait and have that back at camp when he got back.

The trails and road were dry and mostly woodland, but there was enough water around to make the area inviting to all sorts of wildlife, even the orange stripy kind.

About an hour into his hike he felt that he had made the right decision. Already he had come across broken branches with orange fur stuck on them, paw prints in the sandy old tire tracks too big for panther, and one pile of scat that he couldn't imagine being made by anything smaller than a couple hundred pound animal.

After several more hours and no live tiger, actually no live anything, he was once again seriously discouraged. As he finished the loop he began to think of nothing more than the next wondrous bottle that awaited him in camp. By now he had let his guard down and was just booking to get back.

Without warning a large tiger crashed out onto the trail from the brush on his left about 20 yards ahead of him. Apparently it hadn't seen or sensed Karl, and Karl certainly hadn't heard or seen it. Had it been early in his hike, Karl would have had his gun leveled and aimed before the tiger could decide what to do. But now he was distracted and he barely got the gun in both hands before the animal looked at him and let out a roar that shook the forest. Almost instantly, it disappeared back into the brush before he could even swing the barrel in its direction.

"Damn, I must be losing it," Karl said out loud. "Maybe I should retire this big game hunter gig and just open a bar in some war zone or other."

At least he knew they were still out here. It was just going to be a matter of time and he'd have one or two as trophies, he told himself.

By now the depression in the Eastern Atlantic had become strong enough to grab the hurricane watchers' attention. It had become a tropical depression, but it was clearly building and moving westward. It showed every indication that it would build quickly into a tropical storm. If this one developed into a storm to be named it would be called Nana. The trackers hoped the grandmotherly name would portend well for the future impact of this depression.

64

Sitting at a picnic table in the shade looking out over the Smallwood marina and staring at Kim and Saul sat a good looking guy in his mid-thirties. His cap had a logo for one of the Chokoloskee airboat tour companies. Kim had asked if she could take some shots around the area so she was shooting away as Saul asked questions.

"Have you or anyone you know here spotted tigers around?"

"I never saw one, but Elden up the lane there claims he's seen a couple since the incident."

"The incident you mean is when the first man was killed out on Rabbit Key?"

"Yeah, that's the incident I mean. Elden's been out fishing and gator poaching since then more than anyone else I know here, so he was more likely to spot one if they're around."

"You don't seem worried about telling me about him 'gator poaching.' Why is that?"

"Ya see, before this area got more gentrified," the man said, sweeping his arm around and pointing out the small block and tin roofed houses, trailers, and cars and boats in disrepair on blocks around the area, "most folks here made a living in ways that you might say were less than legal."

"Was gator poaching the main activity back then?"

"Not really. It was part of it for sure, but most here were into running drugs for the cartels in Mexico. We're kinda isolated out here so it was easy for the drug folks to meet up with some of the locals offshore and pass on big loads of drugs to take inland."

"What brought about the 'gentrification' as you call it?"

"The feds came in and arrested just about everyone. They were kinda good about it, though, and decided rather than send everyone to prison for long sentences, they would help them rehabilitate by getting them started in the tourist business with Glades tours and fishing charters and such."

"Why would people like Elden go back to the old ways, then, if this was legal and working out for people?"

"See that's just the thing. Once they shut off the tourist trade, we had nothin' out here. It hasn't been very long the park's been closed, but when you more or less live charter to charter like most of us do, you got to find something to bring in the money to live on. Goin' back to gator poaching is the fastest way back. It'll take some doing to re-start the drug running business if it goes on long enough for that to be necessary. By now the drug people have found other places to run their wares through. Comin' back to us isn't high on their lists now."

"Won't the feds be on you again like before?"

"Probably not for a while if they're busy with them tigers and such. Guess we'll have to take our chances if it comes to that."

Once they wrapped the interview and Kim had enough pictures to satisfy her, they headed back to the car.

"Up for some jackpot bingo, writer-man?"

"What?"

"How about we hit the Miccosukee casino on the way back and talk to some of those folks. They live out in the Glades and also run tours. Remember the one where the tourists were dumped off an airboat? That was them."

"Jackpot bingo, huh? Well B 19 has always been a favorite combination of mine. Let's go, shutterfly."

Kim couldn't resist adding, "At least no one will accuse us of doing this story with no reservations."

Saul groaned with appreciation as they got to their car.

65

"I'm finally feeling strong enough and pain-free enough to get back out in the field, and now we seem to be confined to base. If I can't be productive I'm going to head home where I'm sure I have stacks of work to keep me from the boredom."

"Come on, Jake. We can't be out in the field all the time and we just finished moving everyone into the main buildings here from your RVs. Give me a chance to see what's up around the project and we'll get you out there as soon as we can."

"OK, Steve. I'll give it a day or so, but just hanging around here is not getting us any new information and it certainly isn't the most exciting place to spend my time."

"Why Mr. Allnutt, I thought the extensive video library your tax dollars have provided here would be satisfactory to a man of your sensibilities," quipped Shelly/Hepburn.

Jake was aware that even the short quip with the movie reference would have seemed like a put down not long ago and might have set him off, or at least made him angry enough to walk away. But not now.

"It's just that I don't see any of them Spencer Tracy movies in the stack miss, and his are the only ones I really want to watch," Bogart/Jake replied.

And while everyone was smiling, Jake decided to bring up the accommodation issue too.

"Uh, Steve. While I was recuperating I walked all over this place including over the path across the creek, and saw what I take to be staff housing over there. Why aren't we in there if we have to leave our RVs? The places looked pretty comfy to me and it would be a lot better than the locker room amenities and dorm conditions we've set up here."

"They are nice, Jake. But when the park got closed, everyone who was living there had to leave fast and they were told they'd be back in a day or so. No one thought it would be as long as it's been. Those places are full of personal belongings. They really are private homes, so we couldn't just move in there. I know this seems inconvenient but it's not too bad. I mean, we did manage to get your RVs parked adjacent to the buildings with electricity enough to keep them modestly air conditioned so you didn't have to move all your stuff in here. I'm sorry we don't have a way to get you sanitation and water hook ups, too, but it's not that bad."

"Not only is it not bad, but Tonya is so happy to be so much closer to her dinner over here," Randy added.

Jake was still not happy, but he would put up with it for now.

"Besides," Steve continued, "Even though we all haven't made much progress on what you and I have worked on Jake, Randy and Shelly have been finding some surprising and worrisome things lately. You and I will get out there and add even more very soon."

66

Kim and Saul pulled in from their trip beyond the Glades just at dusk. The no-see-ums were ferocious, and no one was out and about. They saw their RV pulled up near the main visitor center as Steve had said it would be in a phone conversation with them. They had stopped for dinner at the same boat rental, gas station, bait shop, and fishing outlet Shelly had been taken to for a meal on her way in here. They too loved the food and the atmosphere. Certainly not Miami chic.

As they walked into the main lobby everyone was gathered around chatting. They all looked up simultaneously, and in voices echoing the greeting for Norm on the TV show "Cheers" shouted, "Media!"

"What did you guys find out there?" Shelly asked.

"A bunch of people who are seriously inconvenienced and really scared by all this tiger business," replied Saul.

"And bunches of people who have run across evidence of them being around but very few actual sightings. The most visuals were reported by the Miccosukee near the resort, but then they live there 24/7 so that would be expected I guess." Kim added. "We heard about the new kill on Route 29 near Corkscrew."

"Yeah that made us expand where we're looking, and I think we are finding some really worrisome trends here," Steve said.

"I've gotten more samples with tiger DNA than I thought I would," said Shelly. "The surprises for me have been that the samples indicate all four types of tigers are out there in numbers, with no real pattern. Even more problematic, positives came from way outside the park. Actually as far north as the Caloosahatchee."

"I have to wonder if any containment we thought we had set up on the wildlife corridor and park perimeters is not working at all," Steve mused.

"Why would you think it's a containment issue those sample represent rather than expecting them to point to new drops from more illegal owners?"

"DNA similarities in some of the samples, Saul," Shelly added.

"That's not all. We've gotten more aerials and satellite photos from areas even north of the Caloosahatchee, and guess what? More trail-like evidence in all kinds of vegetation, suggesting they may be all over the area south of Orlando, particularly along the corridor," Randy added.

"I think we're just damn lucky there have been as few incidents as there have been. I don't see how we're going to get control of this at all," Steve said. "For now, though, we just keep at it while every agency that can be involved gets together to hatch some sort of plan for what happens next."

"Well if they're all the pussy cats Tonya is, why don't we just have every community in Florida set up tiger petting zoos? Just think of the revenue." Saul quipped.

"Just think of the liability insurance, writer-man," Kim said.

67

"Now looky here, Leon, with these dangerous animals seemly all over any place there's a swamp or a tree, I think it's about time we just shut the doors on at least our state parks south of Ft. Meyers and Palm Beach and see if we can't sell that acreage for gated communities, stepped care facilities, malls, and golf courses like we have most of the area along the Gulf Coast. We certainly can use the revenue. Why, hell, even the locals down there would benefit from the taxes which they aren't getting now as long as we keep the parks running." The Governor was on a roll, trying to convince his head of the parks Department of the benefits to shuttering a good portion of the state park system.

"Come on, Governor, you know you can't just do that outright. There are lots of hoops to go through. Besides you'll hear a huge outcry from all sorts of groups from the environmental people to school teachers. In fact you'll hear from any number of people who want the parks left alone or improved."

"Maybe so, Leon, but they'll come around once they see the financial benefit and what's sure to be the decline in tigers eating their friends. And just you watch whether I can do that or not. You're goin' to be real surprised."

"I don't think I can go along with any plan like this, sir."

"You could resign, you know."

"Or you could fire me and we could see what the press does with that."

"Look, what if we leave all the properties open in the Keys. No tigers there that I heard of and maybe the ones that are part of that hallway for critters the environmental people are always on about. That should make it seem like we are just doin' this to protect the big population areas while still keeping places that're good for swamps and tourism."

"It's called the wildlife corridor, sir. And I doubt that any of what you just proposed will keep the shouting down if you try to go ahead with anything like the plan you just described."

"Hey, I haven't seen the feds reopening the Glades or Big Cypress, and Audubon hasn't been rushing to reopen Corkscrew either. What's to say they aren't thinking the same way I am about the future?"

"I just can't get on board with what you are proposing. Maybe we should give it some time and talk again later, sir."

"Or maybe you should just find a way to get on board or find a highway outta town. Whaddya think, Leon?"

"I'll get back to you on which one it will be in a day or so."

"You got an hour and a half. That's how long my meeting with that association of developers is going to take. Let me know which it is. Now send in those boys as you graciously make your exit."

This was a fast moving storm. It had picked up a whole lot of energy and speed in a very short time. By now it was clear that whatever it was about to become it would be taking aim at the Eastern Bahamas first and then…. Well it was too early for the models to predict. One thing for certain, however. With the ocean as hot as it was, this one could become a serious threat.

68

Steve and Jake were heading out in a skiff for the day to survey along the southern border of the park east of the visitor center. They hadn't been out along the Florida Bay side before, and there was a lot of shoreline and an amazing number of islands along this area as they headed east.

The water along here was very shallow, so they had to look out constantly for sandbars. Bottom maps were of marginal help since the sand and marl shifted constantly, changing the underwater landscape.

Besides looking for evidence of tigers, they were also counting the birds, mammals and herps (amphibians and reptiles) they saw. Since it seemed to them that all of these organisms were in frighteningly short supply in the Glades in comparison to what had been there not very long ago, they needed some real numbers to see if their impressions were borne out.

Jake was hoping to see a crocodile, too, while they were out, since he had never seen one in the wild. This was just the place for them, even though there weren't many left around to be seen.

"It's hard to believe that this shallow water is compromising the Glades," Jake said after they had been out for about an hour.

"I know what you mean, Jake. When the storms come in, particularly from the south in the summer and when the tide is high, they really push the saltwater up into the tidal creeks and even flood some of the hammocks and prairies. Look at the vegetation along here and well up into the creeks as we pass the outfalls. Mangroves and other salt tolerants go way back in. The total water flow should be more fresh water out of the Glades rather than saltwater in. That's not happening as much anymore. The sea level has risen now more significantly than anyone had predicted a decade. Anyone who wants to see sea-level rise should come here. We've got it for sure."

"So give me your honest opinion, Steve. Can the Everglades be brought back to what they were?"

"Can anything, Jake? Say we get rid of every invasive species we have here and somehow shore up the coastline around the park, restore the fresh water flow out of the north and get rid of all the nutrient pollution that could come with it. Then what? Will the place just magically recover?"

"Never happened anywhere else, so probably not here either."

"My thoughts exactly. What we may get if all those miracles ever happens is a new normal, a system that gets to some sort of equilibrium that is probably very different from what was here before. It might be recognizable ... but it might not."

"So what are we really doing out here, Steve? I really don't want to just watch over the death of an ecosystem."

"What little we can to keep it alive, my friend. It's the best any of us can do. Change will come, and most of the time how things change will be out of our control. But we can do our best to try and make that change non-lethal."

"Sorry I asked. I could have given you the same answer had you asked me, though. It's pretty much what I tell my students every time they start talking about saving the world. I guess I just needed to hear it from someone like you who spends so much time on the front lines."

After another hour of slow surveying along the coastline, Steve stopped the boat.

"What's that back in the brush by that sandy area, Jake? Can you get the binoculars on it?"

"Good god, it's a camp of some sort. And it looks like it is still in use, not some remnant from before the park was closed."

Steve swung his binoculars into position.

"See anyone around it?"

"No, but look at all that equipment. Whoever's camp that is came out here prepared for a long stay and a whole bunch of different ways to get around the park. I see a boat, a kayak, a trail bike, maybe a motor for it too."

"We'd better get back and let the others know what we've found and maybe get the authorities out here to check it out if they can spare the personnel. You brought your gun with you, didn't you?"

"I've got it but I'm not in the mood to shoot campers just because they jumped the fence."

"I know, I know. We just don't know what this person or these persons are up to and whether they're armed. I just hope they don't start shooting before we get out of here."

Steve fired up the motor, turned the boat around and headed back to Flamingo much faster than they had travelled out to here. Jake's crocodile dreams were taking a back seat now.

What they hadn't noticed was that just as they has stopped their boat a figure in camouflage had started to exit the vegetation and enter the campsite only to stop dead in his tracks when he heard the motor and the voices. Karl had slowly lowered himself to a kneeling position and swung his rifle into firing position. Then he waited.

Once the skiff was out of sight, Karl got to his feet and went into his camp. No evidence the people on that boat had gotten out and come here. They obviously now knew he was here. No sense in hiding any more. Soon time to make some new acquaintances, he thought.

By now the National Hurricane Center had named her Nana. She was a category one storm and about 200 nautical miles east of Eleuthera. The predictive models had come in. So far the models were almost all indicating a storm that would build to a category four or five by the time it hit the Bahamas, and then it would swing dramatically north, missing most of the southeastern coast. The models' paths mostly looked like this storm would hit Wilmington, as so many of the big ones do. Not all models are created equal, however.

69

Kim realized that she had spent very little time shooting at Flamingo. So after breakfast she asked Randy if he would take Tonya for a walk around the whole Center area while she took pictures. She wanted to get Randy and Tonya in as many as she could and she wanted to learn what he was seeing that others had trouble finding. She also didn't want to be out there alone.

After about an hour and a half of walking and talking, they came back inside, sweaty and thirsty.

"Mind if I follow you two until lunch and get some shots of you doing what you do inside here?"

"No problem, Kim. Not a great deal of action from either of us once we get going on the images I get sent. I also think you'll find that Tonya doesn't do very much moving around, either, when we're in here. You should get some good pictures of like, 'Tiger Reclining,' or 'Tiger Snoring,' or 'Tiger Rolling Over' though.

Once they were over by the bank of computers, Kim started shooting away, and true to Randy's predictions, Tonya lay down, rolled over, and went to sleep. It didn't take Kim long to notice that Randy was flagging things on the images he downloaded this morning that didn't seem at all different from any of the other areas of those images.

"What are you looking for, Randy? Can you show me?"

"Sure, Kim."

Randy started with some of the images where the anomalous features were fairly easy to see, once he pointed them out. Then he moved on to images where the anomalies were not at all clear to Kim, even with Randy's patient explanations. The last group of pictures Randy showed her were real mysteries as far as she was concerned. Obviously Randy had a sense of pattern that was much more acute than hers.

"Wow, Randy. You have a very different eye than anyone I've ever met. Ever thought of becoming a photographer?"

"Not really, Kim. I like doing this kind of thing but I don't think making the pictures in the first place would be my dream job."

"Can I get some shots of screens showing the things you are looking for and have you pointing them out or are these images proprietary?"

"I can get you some that are open access images and then you can shoot away. Just don't wake Tonya until lunchtime, OK. She does need her beauty rest."

"Got it. I'll put the camera on silent mode or maybe just set it to play lullabies."

70

Saul had spent the morning over breakfast and afterward interviewing Shelly. He had spent way too little time with her and Randy and really wanted some detail on what she was doing and how she was doing it. He had been surprised at just how clear she had made some of the details of her work. Saul was not a stranger to genetic analysis, but the tools in the field had advanced far faster than he could keep up. Shelly had caught him up to date easily and showed him both the hardware and software of her genetic analysis.

"I really appreciate how clearly you've been able to explain everything, Shelly."

"It's like Richard Feynman said a long time ago, and I paraphrase, 'If you can't explain something in a way that any undergraduate can grasp it easily, you don't really understand it yourself.' I think doing that is what your job as a journalist is all about anyway too, right?"

"Yeah, it is and it seems like I've been talking to a master this morning."

"Why thank you, sir," Shelly replied with a slight bow.

At that point Kim strolled into the makeshift lab.

"Shelly, mind if I shadow you for the afternoon? I want to get some shots of you working on your genetics samples. I haven't gotten lab shots yet."

"No problem. Now that you've given me a heads up, I'll get my makeup people to give me a Julia Roberts makeover. Would you rather I go with a swim suit or a long cocktail dress for the shoot? Of course, I'll change after lunch. Heaven forbid I get peanut butter on my cocktail dress."

"You got any black jeans and Ts? I'll shoot in black and white and make it a Goth layout."

"OK you two," Saul said. "I'll leave you to it this afternoon and I'll interview Randy and Tonya."

"Good luck on the Tonya interview, writer-man. Have you ever interviewed an animal in a coma before? ... I thought not."

71

"Jake and I found out today that apparently we aren't the only people down here in the park."

Steve had called everyone together in the conference room of the center for a quick catch-up on what he and Jake had seen on their trip along the coast of the bay.

"We've known that there have been jumpers getting into the park along most of the edges where there is any kind of population. God knows why they want to, but we never expected anyone to be down here. The closest place that isn't park property is Islamorada, and that's 30 plus miles over water."

"What we saw was really worrisome, too," Jake added.

"There was a camp that looked like it had been used for a while tucked back in the brush along the shore. It looked like whoever was there has been trying to hide from surveillance, overhead or on the water. We just got lucky enough to catch sight of it."

"We didn't see whoever it was that was using the camp, but we did see a lot of equipment. It looks like the people or person is here for the long haul and well stocked." Steve said.

"Any indication what their reason is for being here and for all the secrecy?" Saul asked.

"Not really. But if I had to guess, I'd say whoever it is probably is out here to bag one or more tigers, maybe for the oriental tiger parts trade," Steve answered.

"That could mean a person who is well armed with big game weapons and probably some personal side-arms as well. It looked like they were set to hunt from boat, kayak, on foot and a possibly motorized bike from what we saw. I'd guess whoever it is could be damn dangerous to us as well as to any tigers out there," Jake suggested.

"We called it into the super up at Shark Valley. He indicated they didn't have anyone to spare right at this point and, if we thought we could handle anything that came of it ourselves, he would go with that. He did contact the Coast Guard about it, but they seem to feel the same way so far. It looks like we're on our own for now, anyway," Steve added.

"Unless and until we know otherwise, we need to treat this person or people as a potential threat and be on our guard. Somebody with weapons who has been trying to stay out of sight isn't likely to take kindly to being discovered.

"Same suggestions as before. None of us out alone ever. Minimal or no after dark wandering outside. And if any of us run into this person or people we need to be very cautious," Steve warned sounding a lot more directive than he ever liked to be. Like it or not, he was nervous.

"Steve and I will be armed at all times from now on, so if anything goes down, find us as soon as possible," Jake said.

"I do hope you don't accidently shoot yourself in the foot, Mr. Allnutt. You know how easily that thing goes off," Shelly said pointing to Jake's weapon.

"It is dangerous only in your dainty little hands, Rosie my girl. Why it is positively baby-proof in my gentle grasp."

Hepburn and Bogart continued to lighten an otherwise somber mood.

"Since the pen is mightier than the sword," Saul continued, "I'll just write this guy out of the story and that will be that."

"How do you know it's a guy and how do you know there is just one of them, writer-man?"

"I have my ways, shutterbug. But you get the picture."

Steve was glad everyone was lightening up after he and Jake broke the news. He just hoped the light mood didn't mean that people would start thinking this wasn't a serious concern. He had to get a report of this to park headquarters so they could decide if they needed to alert more local law enforcement to beef up park perimeters until they re-opened the place.

72

Tonight Karl wasn't in any hurry. He had spent the day hiking and once again came up empty. He had no idea why there were so many reports of tigers out here and he couldn't find one to kill. He knew his camp had been spotted by the folks at Flamingo and he would have to deal with that soon enough. He also knew that as long as he had the time, it was in his best interest to do some planning rather than just rush into next steps.

He wiped down as best he could, getting the sweat and remnants of the field off him. After his first couple of drinks he felt like relaxing into his evening. It seemed like a great place for an evening of Bob Marley but he didn't think he could get enough signal out here to let Pandora entertain him over dinner.

He pulled out a beef taco MRE. If only they packed some Dos Equis dark in these field meals. He'd have to send in that recommendation to his veteran's affairs contacts one of these days. Hell, if they could cook without fire in these MREs, they could provide some nice cold tall ones in them too.

By the time dinner was over, so was a major portion of another Gentleman Jack. Early to bed Karl thought through his haze. Maybe he could dream up some plans for what would go down next. He'd better, because he certainly wasn't thinking clearly enough to reason it through at the moment.

Nana slammed into Arthur's Town and Rock Sound at cat four with 135 mph sustained winds. The islands were well prepared and while there were no injuries or loss of life, there was a huge amount of damage to towns and settlements. It would take years to recover completely. Having passed those islands, most of the predictive models indicated that Nana would be turning north very quickly. Only one predictive model path suggested it might stay on a course that would bring it to Florida and the Everglades. No one thought much of that one little line on the model map. It was being predicted by perhaps the least reliable model in the system. That model hadn't predicted anything correctly in the 30 years it had been in use. Wilmington started to brace for the worst.

73

Being confined more to the indoors at night meant that the campfire ambience they had gotten used to at the end of their days changed dramatically. It didn't stop the flow of wine and beer or the conversation but sitting in real chairs in air conditioning with real lights all around made it all feel like the end of a dinner party rather than a camp sing-a-long.

That meant that the conversation took turns away from the situation at hand and let them range broadly to books, movies, culture, pop and otherwise, and even to politics and religion briefly. Even with those taboo topics, it became clear quickly that this band of strangers thrown together in pursuit of the facts about a most unexpected set of events had far more in common than any of them might have considered likely at the beginning. Even so, there were enough disparate opinions bandied about to keep the energy up for some good give and take. Finally, though, the conversation wound back around to their current situation.

"When do you think we'll get to meet this person or these people who are out here near us?" Saul asked.

"Your guess is as good as anyone's, Saul. I just think we need to be patient and let them come to us rather than surprising them by going back out and introducing ourselves. If they come to us, it might keep things more comfy for us to meet them as a group rather than just one or two of us at a time."

"Steve, do you think I could get close enough to their camp to get some pictures with a good long lens, even if we haven't met them yet?"

"I really don't think it's a good idea to try, Kim. If they're hostile they won't take kindly to clandestine photos being taken and if they're friendly, doing that without asking could set them on the path to being hostile. They'll likely come to us. I'd bet any money they know we're here even if we didn't know they were there."

"Apart from the human issue, with all the evidence for tigers all over the Glades and well beyond that Randy is finding, I just can't imagine why we haven't run into more of the animals."

"I know what you mean, Jake. When I first did a piece for the paper on the python problem, though, I remember hearing how many were out here and how few were ever seen or caught. The best evidence for them seemed to be the havoc they have been causing in the mammal, bird and gator populations. You just told us that you seem to be seeing even more devastation in those populations where you and Steve were looking. Maybe they're trying to avoid people and make a living out there."

"Well it can't be sustained much longer if that's the case, based on what Jake and I saw when we went east. That little excursion turned out to be a 'Silent Late Summer.' It was eerie without the birds, let me tell you."

74

Karl had developed something of a plan. He would take his boat loaded with all sorts of gear to the Snake Bight entrance to Christian Point Trail. There he would load up with ammo and gear and hike into the cut over to Flamingo Road and from there across the dock path across Buttonwood Creek to the visitor center. With his stealth he could do it all unseen and then wait for the perfect time to drop in on whoever was over there and introduce himself. He could then let them see first-hand that he would be in charge from then on. He would then use the center as home base. If it all went well, he would get no resistance -- or little enough that he could nip it in the bud easily.

If there was anyone there that knew where there were tigers he could dispatch, he would bag some he could carry out and be gone back across the bay before any law enforcement or park people could catch up with him. He was still confident that the governor would help him if he needed it, even though he wasn't sure whether the governor knew he was out here in the first place.

The plan felt like a military operation. Enough so that he got that excellent high he remembered when the adrenalin started pumping. He was sure his plan was foolproof and he was invincible.

It appeared that Nana hadn't seen the models at the National Hurricane Center. She decided that she'd just go her own way. So rather than turning north as she was supposed to, she swung west along a path that would take her over Homestead, the main entrance to the Everglades, and the road to Flamingo. She decided she'd keep her cat four status for the first part of the trip anyway.

75

When they had first heard about Nana, Steve had talked to the superintendent and discussed whether it would be best for them to stay on at Flamingo or head out of the park. They agreed that Flamingo was now pretty hurricane resistant; after Wilma and Katrina and taken out a good portion of it, the facilities had been seriously re-outfitted. Those two had come in from the Gulf and left Flamingo without guest accommodations. There had been plans to add new ones but once they got the visitor center up to snuff, the funds and the will had waned. So as long as Nana was going to head up the coast to Wilmington, there was no need to leave. At least that had been the decision during the conversation.

Later Randy came into the main lobby where everyone was gathered from the computer room with Tonya trailing close behind.

"Has anyone else been looking at the weather?"

No one had been.

"I just now checked the National Hurricane Center site and that cat four storm that was going to hit Wilmington just turned after glancing past Nassau and is headed to Homestead and the entrance to the park."

"Whoa, I thought you said it was going to miss us altogether, Steve."

"All the models said it would, Kim."

"All but one and that's the path she decided to take," Randy said.

"Shouldn't we get out of here then?"

"Look Shelly, if we try to drive out of here we would be heading right into the teeth of that storm rather than getting away from it. The center here is probably the best place to be even if it strengthens. This place really is hurricane proof."

"Strengthening seems unlikely, Steve, since these storms mostly lose strength once they hit land. All their energy comes from hot water."

"Which seems to be what we're in now, doesn't it, Jake?"

"What about taking a boat and getting across the bay to the Keys?"

"Probably possible, Saul, particularly if she stays north into the heart of the Glades but there might be enough wind to drive some pretty heavy seas. I still think we're better off just staying put. We've got food, water, power and backup and a building that is rated to cat four plus. Think of it as just another little adventure."

"What about the Glades themselves, and for that matter, the tigers?"

"I've worked out here a lot of years, Saul. The Glades will recover given a chance. With the rise in sea level we've seen down here, storm surge could drive salt water way up into the park. But if enough rain falls up there, it could balance it out, mostly. The tigers and all the other critters out here are another story."

"Animals are amazing at detecting oncoming storms and other events and changing their behaviors to maximize their survival," Jake pointed out. "There are all manner of stories of animals that somehow knew the Indonesian tsunami was coming long before any of the people did and headed for the mountains. Lots of them survived because of that."

"I'd like to be with them," Shelly said.

While the group was discussing the oncoming storm, Karl had slipped in and as quietly as he could, surveyed the building, noting its layout. He had been around the outside of the building before he entered through a window in a storeroom. He had severed the communication lines he had come across as he went. When he got to the computer room he had taken all the power cords and connections from every electronic device he had found and put them in a janitor's closet he had found which had a key in the lock. He'd kept the key. He was sure that everyone who was in the building was in the main room because he hadn't seen any sign of anyone other than them on site.

Karl stepped quietly out of shadows on the far side of the room where everyone was gathered. He was armed to the teeth and looked like a special ops soldier ready for his mission. The rifle was not pointed at anyone in particular but it seemed very much at the ready as Shelly spotted him and gasped.

"'Evenin' y'all. Pleased ta make your acquaintance. My name's Karl. You can call me 'sir.' And as the man said in the movie, 'I'm da captain now!'"

76

Nana was a tight storm for the cat three she remained as she made landfall on the mainland not far from Homestead. Her hurricane force winds extended out only about 80 miles from her eye. She carried massive amounts of water. The winds and the water were going to take out trees, roads and trailer parks all along her path. The team at Flamingo had been wise to stay put because they would have driven right into the middle of that destruction along the main park road which was soon to become impassable.

While Karl's military training had taught him to expect the unexpected, he was struck by two things immediately that weren't in his planning book. There were two people standing in the room with side arms and, unbelievably, a kid with his hand on the neck of a live tiger.

Karl snapped his rifle into firing position, aiming first at the tiger. As he did that Randy, seemingly anticipating Karl's move, pushed Tonya toward an open archway to the cafeteria as he dropped and rolled in the opposite direction. Somehow Tonya got the message and headed through the archway at top speed. In that fraction of a second Jake had managed to pull his pistol and fired toward Karl but missing him. Even so, the explosion of the 44 distracted Karl just enough that his shot missed the fleeing tiger.

By now Steve had his weapon out and opened fire over Karl's head with several shots as he yelled for everyone to scatter and take cover. Karl was now facing the possibility of shots coming at him from two different directions and that meant he had to make a split second decision which way to shoot. That small window gave the team an instant to scatter and get to other rooms. Even Steve and Jake were almost out of the room before Karl got off his next barrage of shots.

Now Karl was faced with choices. He could go after any one or even two of the people he had seen scatter but he couldn't go after all of them at once. The safari man with the cannon pistol had gone in one direction and the guy in the Smokey the Bear uniform had gone in another. He was being flanked and he needed to figure out how to minimize his risk. The rifle wasn't going to be the best weapon for indoor work but he didn't want to jettison it either. So he slung it on his back, drew his machine pistol and paused to make his decision. He knew the tiger would have to wait until he regained better control. Once he did, though, he would finally be assured of bagging at least one tiger.

Outside, the winds were picking up to 35 mph and gusting. Rain bands swept through the area. Nana hadn't lost much of her punch yet, but she was swinging north finally, probably headed appropriately to Dismal Key. She would be dropping a lot of rain, and there would be increasing winds all through the Glades, all the way out into Florida Bay, and over to Islamorada.

What no one could have seen, however, was the movement of eight of the tigers that had been wandering in the southern part of the Glades. While coming in from very different directions, they were all moving toward the visitor center. For them this day, that building had served as their mountains of Banda Aceh.

77

Steve found himself in an office with only the door back out into the main room as an access. There was a window that looked out on a paved area where some equipment for the boats was stored. He could see the wind and rain pummeling the area. The good news was that if this guy came for him he would have only one way to get in and Steve would have the first shot since Karl wouldn't know where Steve was in the room. He thought he knew, probably from watching too much TV as a kid, that when entering a room in pursuit you had to look quickly left and right. So he chose to crouch low behind the desk square onto the door with his pistol aimed about belly height dead center of the opening.

Jake had dived right behind Tonya into the cafeteria. Tonya had run to the back behind the steam table so Jake stayed low and crawled there too.

Shelly and Kim were in the mail room, which opened out into a back office. They had crawled there and found a hallway exit that they took. Neither really knew where it led, but farther away was better, as far as they were concerned.

Somehow Saul and Randy found themselves back in the lab space Shelly had set up. They had no idea where to go from there. Just not moving for a few seconds so they could let their hearts slide back down from their throats to their chests seemed about all they could do.

Karl decided to go for the room he saw the guy in the safari clothes disappear into. That one only had a revolver and therefore only six shots before he had to reload. That is if he had more than six bullets with him. This had gone a lot worse than he had thought it could. Who would have expected armed environmentalists and a tiger all in one room? Time to get control.

Shelly and Kim worked their way along the hall until they found a door that they were sure went into the lab. Shelly cracked the door as quietly as she could hoping not to see Karl when she did. What she saw were Randy's sneakers sticking out from behind one of her makeshift lab benches. There was no sign of Karl. She opened the door a bit more and found Saul staring her way apparently having heard the slightest squeak of the hinges. She motioned for him and Randy and they crawled almost on their bellies into the hallway with Kim and Shelly. Shelly closed the door as silently as she could. Using hand signals only, they decided to move down the hall in the opposite direction to how Shelly and Kim had come. None of them knew what was there but it just didn't seem like staying still was an option.

Winds were up to 50 mph by now outside. There had been enough rain that the southern Glades was a true river of grass once again, if only briefly. The Bay was alive with waves crashing against sea walls and docks and tossing small boats out of the water here and there around the center's marina. The eight tigers were getting closer to the center. None of them knew as yet that they were not alone. Each just knew somehow that there might be salvation in that place where there had been people not so long ago.

78

Karl had settled into his combat mode. More clear-headed now, he had quickly decided that he needed to take a hostage to get all the others in the building to surrender to him. He had come to the realization that he really didn't need to kill anyone unless it became absolutely necessary for self-defense. Maybe he was becoming soft, but it might also go better should the worst happen and he got caught. Then he wouldn't have a homicide charge facing him along with all the other charges he would garner. "Since when have I become such a nice guy?" he asked himself.

Saul pulled his notebook and pencil out of his pocket and on a blank page wrote, **EXIT** ⟹

He held the page up to the group in the hall so the arrow was pointing to a heavy door just down the hall from where they had stopped crawling in order to take a breather. Everyone nodded even knowing that if they opened that door they would be facing driving rain and horrible winds.

Shelly signaled for the pad and pencil and on a clean page wrote,

JAKE & TONYA FIRST.

The other three signaled OK and they continued crawling past the exit door. They finally came to a door leading to the room they believed Jake and Tonya were hiding. Shelly wrote on the pad, **J&T COME WITH US**.

This time Randy took the initiative to crack open the door, thinking that if Tonya saw him she would come to him right away and maybe Jake would follow even if he couldn't see the note. Whether the door made enough noise for Tonya to hear it or not, by the time Randy had the door open enough to see in, Tonya was right beside it staring at him. As Randy opened the door just a little wider Jake beat Tonya through it but the tiger was close behind.

At that moment Karl rushed in diving and rolling and coming up in firing position just a fraction of a second too late to see Tonya's tail slip through the quietly closing door.

Everyone in the hall froze. It seemed only logical that once Karl didn't see Jake or Tonya in the room he would realize that they had run. He would search the space, find this door, and be on them in a heartbeat. What they didn't know was that the door they had used was actually one of three in the back of the cafeteria. Once Karl realized his quarry had slipped out somewhere, he did head for the nearest door to where he had landed when he dove in. It wasn't theirs.

As soon as the band in the hall realized that Karl had started off in the wrong direction, Saul once again put up his exit message with the arrow pointing to the outside door.

Jake, understanding how communication was going down out here grabbed the pad and wrote, **STEVE**!

Kim grabbed the pad and wrote, **COULDN'T FIND DOOR**. Jake took the pad and wrote, **WINDOW?**

Several of the group shrugged and then they began crawling to the exit door. When Saul opened that door they were greeted with needles of rain being hurled at them as they crawled outside, stood as best they could and pressed their bodies as close to the building as they could. Even Tonya seemed to know what to do. They were sure the sound of the storm through the open door would attract Karl and they would soon be in trouble again as well as soaking wet and bruised.

Tigers are solitary. But three of the eight heading to the visitor center had found each other during their push through the storm, sometimes swimming in the rising river of grass. When they met, rather than challenge each other or flee, they had begun moving as a group, a tiger pack. Not what tigers do.

79

Karl was getting very frustrated. He had checked all three doors in the back of the cafeteria and there was no one behind any of them. He had found the one to the hallway but when he got into it he had a clear view end to end and he saw no one. There were other doors into the space along its length but he had no idea where they went and he needed to get at least someone under control soon. The last person he wanted to tackle for this part of his plan was the Smokey with the pistol. He would have a clip with a lot more than six shots and maybe more than one clip. He'd have to take him out completely if it came to that.

He saw a door that appeared to lead outside. It looked like the storm had breached that one since the floor was wet around it. He didn't really want to go out there unless he had to. He made the decision to take the last door in the hall. It was the one to the lab. Maybe coming at them from behind he could surprise the two guys who were in there and take them both in one smooth operation. This could be fun.

The windblown and rain-beaten band of six hugging the wall of this big pink building slid down past where they imagined the hallway they had escaped ended. There was only one window beyond it, right on a corner of the building. Around that corner lay some big trees. At least there were big trees there before the storm began. And beyond them the marina.

Almost without needing to communicate the plan to each other the group had come to the realization that the only way out now was to get to the water and hope they could maneuver through the chaos of the Bay waters in whatever vessel that could carry them all that was still afloat. They weren't going without Steve if they could help it.

Jake was the first to the window and peered carefully around the casement. Even through the sheets of water pouring down the glass he could make out Steve hunkered behind a desk in the office. Risking being heard again, Jake gave as gentle a tap on the window as he could still making enough of a sound to be heard. Steve swung around with his gun in his hand and barely refrained from shooting at the sound of the tap.

Once Jake signaled, Steve was up and over to the window. He knew the minute he opened the window enough noise would roar in that Karl would know he was headed outside and be in there in a flash. His escape was going to be all about speed.

Everyone was surprised at just how fast Steve was able to almost simultaneously open the window and dive out tucked for a roll. He was on his feet almost instantly. As the seven of them rounded the corner of the building, Karl burst into the office where Steve had been, firing randomly. He had decided that the man in that room would probably not hesitate to shoot him first if he could so he decided to scratch his original plan and shoot away. He'd come up with some excuse for the kill later if he needed to. The room was empty but the window was open and the storm was pouring in.

By now the winds were down a bit but the rain was still fierce. More of the eight tigers had joined the group, a unique and unprecedented pack. They were closing in on the visitor center.

80

Now that they were out of the building they could talk to each other again. With the noise of the wind they had to speak louder than any of them wanted to but they need a plan of action and fast with Karl surely breathing down their necks.

"I think the only way out of here now is by boat," Steve said. "The road will be washed out and covered with debris for days. I just hope we have one down there big enough for all of us and good enough to fight the seas we're about to get ourselves into."

"Tonya and I saw one of the big tour boats anchored near one of the outside docks facing the Bay, Randy said. "If it's still there, it's probably the biggest and best shot we've got."

"I wish you wouldn't use the word shot just now," Shelly said.

"I thought it seemed very appropriate, Rosie," Jake responded.

"This is not the time for that crap," Saul said tersely.

"Got it," Jake replied.

They raced as fast as they could toward the dock, having trouble seeing their way in the rain, and maneuvering around downed trees and other debris, some of which was still being blown around and becoming airborne as they moved.

Karl had had enough. He climbed out the window of the office and made his way around the building, having not seen anyone along the wall that ran along the outside of the interior hall. By the time he spotted the group they were almost to the water. Karl saw immediately where they were headed. A tour boat was there bouncing up and down in the crashing waves but looking unlikely to capsize or be carried onshore. That's where they were going.

Karl knew that his sidearm was not the weapon of choice out here now at this distance in this weather so he pulled the big game rifle back over his shoulder and fired a few shots in the direction of the fleeing group. He hit no one but he always felt better when he was shooting a powerful weapon.

When the seven got to the boat Steve grabbed the wheel and found enough purchase to start the engine. Amazingly, it turned over immediately. The others all tried to steady themselves in the lurching boat. Tonya lay flat between the rows of seats and was thrown back and forth across the aisle getting bruised but not seriously injured. Everyone else just held on best they could as Steve found a way to get the boat untethered and moving to what passed for open water in this very shallow bay. Water clarity was zero so there was every possibility that they would wind up on a sand bar any minute. He would head toward the Keys and hope for the best.

Karl moved out from the building into an open paved area that was covered in downed limbs and debris blown in from all over the area. He gave up trying to deal with those fools now. He figured they would all drown on their way to wherever they thought they were going, and he couldn't care less. He was now alone in the Glades with the tigers. He could kill as many as he wanted. He was going to be a rich man once he got those animal parts to the oriental medicine traffickers. He was looking forward to quitting the King Ranch gig and maybe retiring to Belize.

The tigers had just made it to the center. They were a pack of eight now. With silent communication they spotted Karl and split into four groups of two. Tigers don't plan or strategize. Or do they?

A battered and bent tour boat limped into the inlet just north of Route 1 by Islamorada Tarpon Fishing. How they had made it there they weren't entirely sure, but Steve had managed the boat in the storm better than anyone could have imagined. Everyone was beaten up and bruised, but now that the boat was in calm protected water inside this inlet, they were also smiling. It had been a hell of a ride.

Two days later Steve gathered the seven of them together in the bar at the Amara Cay Resort, the only place they could find on Islamorada that allowed tigers. Well, not really, but they allowed this one.

"We got the Coasty report from their flyover of Flamingo. The building is intact but no sign of life anywhere. They did take some pictures. The only thing of note was one of a rifle that was just lying out on the tarmac beside the building. Nothing else."

THE GOVERNOR

"How could those idiots reopen all those federal lands with tigers out there? Have they no feeling for the safety of the public? Besides, what will this do to my plans for keeping the state parks and such closed and redeveloped? God this cat thing continues to be incredibly annoying! And it's taking way too much of my time."

"First of all, the feds have all sorts of dangerous situations in their parks and monuments," Leon explained. "About 150 people die in those properties every year. Not all because of dangers in the parks themselves but certainly plenty of those. Tigers just add a new and relatively unknown problem for the Glades," he said.

"I don't want those effete environmental types suing the state when one of them gets eaten out there, my friend. I have every mind to keep the damn state properties closed forever."

"I still think you not only shouldn't do that, sir. I don't think you legally can do that alone. Maybe if you got the state legislature to buy into it, but not by mandate. I think the legislature isn't likely to back you on that any time soon."

"I knew I should have fired you before you decided to stay on."

"Not only the feds are reopening, though. Audubon has already reopened Corkscrew since Nana pretty much missed them."

"Isn't that lovely. I hope the tigers eat all their birds and they're left with boxcar loads of bird seed. Now I gotta convince those developer guys that what I promised them wasn't really a promise. I can't wait 'til I'm outta here and up in Washington where money talks louder than people."

"Anything you say, sir," Leon said turning and walking out of the governor's office.

STEVE

"Thanks for stopping by, Steve," said the superintendent as Steve walked through the door.

"My pleasure, Chief. What's up?"

"To get right to the point, I want to congratulate you on your promotion. You're now Assistant Superintendent of Everglades National Park. A good bump in salary, too. And you deserve it for what you've done for the park with the tiger issue."

"I wish I felt that what I'd done had been a success, though. They're still out there in numbers and the park is still reeling with the consequences. Anyway, thanks. How does this change my day-to-day?"

"Now that the park is back open with a whole range of new rules for safety, what we would like for you to do is head up all the efforts to keep the public as safe as we can with the new normal. Just so you don't get bored, we also are putting you in charge of all the studies and remediation planning for all of the invasive species we have out there. It'll be an enormous job and with the expected federal cutbacks under this administration, you'll have to do it on practically zero budget."

"Gee, that sounds like fun! Are you sure this is a promotion?"

"I get the sarcasm, Steve, but we do need you out there. If it's any consolation, you'll get a nicer office even though you might not be in it very much."

"Given a choice, I'd rather not be in it at all, thank you. But there you go."

"To add to your worries Steve, I know you are aware that there are a crap load of big cats out there as part of the exotic pet trade that are just unaccounted for. The people in Washington think that the only reason we are seeing only tiger out here so far is that the other cats' owners haven't formed groups and coalitions like the tiger owners did. They expect that to change and we may see a whole range of species dumped in our park and others once those owners all get organized. Are you ready to tackle lions and leopards and jaguars? Hope so because they're telling me that's what may be coming our way next."

Steve paused to let it all sink in. "Hear me roar, sir," Steve said with a smile that might have been more of a grimace. "I'll give it my best shot."

"I know you will. And if it means anything, what you do now will make your job a lot easier when you are behind this desk in the not too distant future."

KIM AND SAUL

While there had been many stories written in the media during the tiger episode, all of them had been straight-forward news articles reporting facts that cropped up along the way and quoting a wide variety of people, players and non-players alike. When Kim and Saul's first feature came out with an in-depth look at the events at Flamingo and beyond, it added a much needed dimension that began to tie the whole story of tigers in America to the plight of the Everglades and the entire exotic pet trade.

That story had gotten such traction that they were soon approached about a book deal from a publisher in Chicago. Their editor and the top brass were happy to give them the time to write and promote it as long as the paper got a lot of publicity in the process.

When a documentary film company approached them about a feature-length film following up on the original saga and where the work would go from here, they once again jumped at the opportunity with the blessing of the paper's higher-ups. They figured that they could work on both projects simultaneously.

They were enjoying continuing to work together and they were very much looking forward to all of the opportunities this would provide to be back in touch with the Flamingo team they had come to care so much about. They had even started talking more about future features on some of the more interesting people they had encountered on this story. They would have plenty of time to talk it all through, too, on that dive vacation they booked together to the Bay Islands.

RANDY AND TONYA

What can you do with tiger like Tonya in New York City? Nothing reasonable. So that was why once Tonya had been thoroughly checked over by vets in Florida, Randy had found a way to get her transported to Popcorn Park, a zoo and sanctuary in New Jersey that had agreed to take her. It wasn't ideal. She wouldn't roam free or have hands-on contact with any of the staff, but she would be safe, well fed, and have good medical care. It was less than two hours from the city and that had become an important consideration.

Randy had come back to the museum after some much needed family time in Maine to find that Shelly and several others had gone to bat with everyone they knew to get him a paid position, and it had worked. He would float among the labs as an in-house analyst looking for previously unrecognized patterns in data from studies ranging from biofilms to dinosaurs.

He was delighted. He had quickly found an apartment in Newark that he could afford. That even put him closer to Tonya whom he would visit as often as possible. He hoped that would be on most weekends and at least one evening mid-week. The museum even was willing to consider flex time or a four-day work week if he wanted it, and working remotely was possible too. He had proven that at Flamingo. If that worked out, he could spend even more time with Tonya.

So far the park staff seemed to turn their backs when he showed up and he had managed to find a way to get into the enclosure with Tonya. No park in their right mind would allow that to happen because of the liability. But no one knew, right? And both Randy and Tonya were delighted with the arrangement so far, but he wanted very much to be with this big cat full time. He would find a way, he promised himself.

JAKE

Jake had been on what seemed to be a treadmill since getting back home. He had stacks of paper to deal with in the office, a passel of students like Mike he needed to follow up with and keep directed on productive paths. He would deal with the loss of his camper and truck, write up reports for all the administrative levels of the university, and try to get into some of the data he and his students had collected over the field season just ended. He couldn't imagine how he would have dealt with it all if he had to teach a full load this semester, too. He was really grateful for his leave.

Jake had found the time to get together with his colleague who was head of the university's "Panther Posse" and offer his services whenever he could. He even felt as if he would find a way to shift his research focus to a Florida panther project, but that move was way down the line for now. He also hoped that somewhere down the road he could wind up working with Steve again. He had come to respect him as a scientist and ranger, and he had become a good friend in the bargain.

Jake would have thought that he was going to be too busy and engaged with detail to think about the people he had worked with in the Glades. He would have been wrong. He thought of them often. He knew what each team member had brought to the tiger effort. Jake had never worked on a committee or a team that functioned so well together and who all even seemed to like each other in the end.

That had not been the case for Jake early on. Except for Steve and maybe Randy, Jake had found each of the other team members assembled at Flamingo got on his nerves and seemingly worked counter to what he thought would have been best practices. The one that had really set him off at the beginning was Shelly, and Jake had been put off by what he perceived as her rather superior attitude about almost everything. He was even a bit put off by what he had to admit had been a couple of losing exchanges of snarky comments between them in the early going. By the end, though, he had developed a serious respect and more of a fondness towards Shelly than he had expected he could.

And so tonight, with a healthy dram of single malt in hand, Jake was sitting in his favorite chair listening to some quiet smooth jazz, staring into space and trying not to think about anything. Almost without thinking, he reached for the phone and he found himself punching in a number he had been sure he would never call. He thought about hanging up as soon as the ringing started, but for some reason he just couldn't. He had no idea what he was going to say if the call was answered but … what the hell.

SHELLY

The hustle and noise of New York City had seemed jarring at first after all that quiet in the Glades, but it still felt like home to Shelly in so many ways. It hadn't taken her long to settle back into her routine at the museum and socializing with friends, but she was often brought up short by an intense sense that she was missing something. And that something was something she never thought she could miss: what John Muir meant when he wrote, "In every walk with nature one receives far more than he seeks."

Tonight, like most nights, Shelly had gotten home late after a stop at a bodega for some supplies for dinner and another stop at her favorite local wine shop to pick up the owner's recommendation for her this week. She had collected a stack of books at the New York Public Library earlier in the week and after a dinner that included two generous glasses of the very good cab the wine store owner had suggested, she settled in for an evening of sorting through her stack to see what she would start reading tonight.

Shelly had been surprised how much she missed the people she had come to know in the Everglades. Initially she wrote it off as "summer camp" friendships that wouldn't last much longer than the seemingly sincere promises to keep in touch when the project was finally over. But in short order, she started to realize that she really respected the team she had become a part of and cared a lot about each and every one.

She had surprised herself by buying some things she really didn't think she needed just because of the impact these folks had on her. Her new digital SLR camera sat on her bookshelf and would be used often. She had started carrying a small notebook for reminders of interesting observations or ideas she encountered. How different from the electronic notes she used to take on her phone. She had checked out natural histories and even an ecology book this go around at the Public. Jake had recommended the one she decided she couldn't wait to start. John Vaillant's "The Tiger" was an appropriate choice for several reasons.

As she picked up her book and opened to the pictures of the Siberian wilderness, her phone rang. Shelly couldn't have been happier when she saw the caller i.d., and that too took her by surprise. She reached over to the end table for the drover hat she had bought a few days ago, placed it jauntily on her head and hit the talk button.

"Why it is just lovely to hear from you, Charlie Allnutt! I was so hoping you would call."

EPILOGUE

The boys had left Folkston, Georgia and driven the short distance to the Davis Lake Boat Landing near Duck Island on the Eastern edge of the Okefenokee, the junction of the Florida and Georgia wildlife corridors. Davis Lake and a few others like it are home to some of the biggest largemouth bass outside the Okefenokee. The access area has just enough room for a car to turn around. It is tucked back into vegetation out of sight and sound of the chicken farm buildings less than a quarter mile away. The red truck had been parked there for about an hour, windows open. The boys had made their way out onto the pond in a small fishing boat with a small quiet motor and were now out of sight of the truck. The owner's yellow lab had been asleep in the shade of the truck for that hour waiting for the boys to get back. He was always in the way on the boat but he never wanted to be left behind when his owner left the house. He was good at waiting, though. He had water and shade. What more could he need.

Boredom took over and the lab sauntered over to the water's edge for a drink and look. There wasn't much to explore but then the dog was ten years old and didn't need to explore too much anyway while he waited. He just wanted to see what there was around.

As he approached the edge of the opening to the water where the boat had been launched, he failed to notice the movement of the nearby vegetation that was different from what you might expect in a breeze. Besides, there was not a breath of air moving back here. He didn't smell anything peculiar either, not that he could have very well with the disruption to his smeller that his owner's smoking had caused over the years.

As the lab got nearer the bushes, the movement in the undergrowth became explosive. In an instant the dog and whatever else had been there were gone. What was left to see were three large wet pug marks drying in the sun, soon to disappear.

QUESTIONS FOR EXPLORATION AND DISCUSSION

1. Do you think there might be tigers in the Everglades? If so, how might they survive?

2. Knowing that the invasive Burmese pythons has destroyed more than 90 percent of the Everglades' mammals and is making a dent in its bird populations, how do you think the introduction of a new large predator might impact the Everglades ecosystem?

3. What are wildlife corridors, and why are they essential to the preservation of species?

4. How does the exotic pet industry impact the ecology of countries from which animals are taken and that of those where they are imported?

5. What does a museum re-constructor like Shelly do? What does their work contribute to our understanding of animals past and present?

6. What are the legitimate concerns of a government when a situation such as this arises? How might officials consider competing issues such as public safety, tourism, economic impact, and the short- and long-term effects on the environment?

7. How might this story be different if Tonya had not become part of it?

8. Jake and Shelly start out mistrustful of each other. What are the bases for their initial mistrust and for their eventual connection?

9. Saul and Kim are quiet, observational journalists. How might they have changed the dynamic with the team if they had been more aggressive in their pursuit of stories and photos?

10. How do Karl's actions reflect what you know about the origins of his character?

ACKNOWLEDGEMENTS

Any book, but particularly a work of fiction, must pass the test of appeal to potential readers. I would like to thank the following first readers for their thoughtful suggestions and comments, which provided invaluable help in shaping this work: David Pindel, Jack Anderson, Deb Rines, Jimmy Schmal, Penny Wilson, Colleen Lilley, Michael and Elke Beykirch, Peggy Brill and David Higgins. Detailed reading and editing suggestions by Heather McGrath, Joann Schmal, Mike Shalter, and Laura McGrath saved me from leaving too many errors in this book. What errors remain are mine alone.

I am blown away by the incredible encouragement that my family has given me throughout the process. Heather, Colleen, and Ted have been wonderful cheerleaders. None of this could have happened without the support and continual honest evaluation and insights from my favorite writer, Laura. I can't express how lucky I feel having you by my side for these many years.

ABOUT THE AUTHOR

For 43 years, Tom McGrath was a professor of biology at Corning Community College, where he taught college biology, genetics, and field courses; developed creative approaches to teaching; directed the college's honors program, and was the first professor in the State University of New York system to be awarded both the Chancellor's Award for Excellence in Teaching and the Chancellor's Award for Excellence in Scholarship and Professional Activity.

Tom was also an active researcher. He developed and served as principal investigator for The Bahamian Reef Survey, which was sponsored by Earthwatch Institute. He published numerous scientific papers on that research and delivered presentations at Oxford University (in the same hall where Darwin once lectured!), Harvard University, the American Museum of Natural History, the Smithsonian National Museum of Natural History, the Norwalk Aquarium, and numerous other venues for a wide variety of audiences.

But Tom's interests are broad, and two of his defining characteristics are his voracious curiosity and unstoppable humor. He is an avid reader, an inveterate punster, a sometime birdwatcher, and a keen photographer. In times past, he has been involved with more than 20 amateur theater productions as an actor, director, or producer; sung in a barbershop quartet; led nature hikes, and created the family vacation motto: "Maximize the experience!"

He now lives in St. Petersburg, Florida and has spent some time exploring the Everglades and other nearby ecosystems. He and his wife feel astonishingly lucky to be live near their children and their charming and brilliant (of course) granddaughter, Marlo.

Tom is happy to speak on the biology of the Everglades and the science embedded in this novel, and also to talk with book groups. He can be reached at Tom.McGrath.stpete@gmail.com.

Made in the USA
Middletown, DE
05 November 2019